'Mum . . . ?' said .....
'Something . . . happened. Something scary . . . I was drawing, and I drew this face, and it went all horrible, and . . . and then it winked at me.'

When she's fed up, Enna doodles. This time it's a scribbly, hunchbacked, squatting figure—which suddenly winks, speaks, and jumps off the page. It's alive, with a mind of its own. Enna can't believe what is happening. Her mother is far too busy and too worried about the café to talk to her, so Enna has to cope on her own—and then her little brother finds the doodle . . . and disappears! What is Enna to do when no one will listen to her? How can she get her brother back? And can the doodle help? Is it all imagination? Or will it lead her into dangers and adventures that she hasn't dreamed of yet?

Philip Gross was born in Cornwall in 1952, the son of an Estonian wartime refugee and a Cornish schoolmaster's daughter. He has won several prizes for his poetry and his collection *The Wasting Game* was shortlisted for the Whitbread Poetry Prize in 1998. He now teaches Creative Writing at Bath Spa University College and lives in Bristol. His first novel for Oxford University Press, *Going For Stone*, is a thrilling and chilling adventure for teenagers. *Marginaliens* shows that he can work magic for s........

Marginaliens

OTHER OXFORD BOOKS BY PHILIP GROSS

Going For Stone

Marginaliens

Philip Gross

OXFORD
UNIVERSITY PRESS

OXFORD
UNIVERSITY PRESS

Great Clarendon Street, Oxford OX2 6DP

Oxford University Press is a department of the University of Oxford.
It furthers the University's objective of excellence in research, scholarship,
and education by publishing worldwide in

Oxford New York
Auckland Bangkok Buenos Aires
Cape Town Chennai Dar es Salaam Delhi Hong Kong Istanbul
Karachi Kolkata Kuala Lumpur Madrid Melbourne Mexico City Mumbai
Nairobi São Paulo Shanghai Taipei Tokyo Toronto

Oxford is a registered trade mark of Oxford University Press
in the UK and in certain other countries

British Library Cataloguing in Publication Data available

ISBN 0 19 271943 2

1 3 5 7 9 10 8 6 4 2

Typeset by AFS Image Setters Ltd, Glasgow

Printed in Great Britain by
Cox & Wyman Ltd, Reading, Berkshire

Chapter 1

A Nod and a Wink

It was stupid. A silly thought—a crazy one—the kind her friends would laugh at if she mentioned it at school. Enna couldn't believe she'd even thought it . . . so she looked back at the notebook just to show herself how silly it had been.

And she gasped. The silly, crazy thought . . . was true.

The thing in the notebook was watching her.

But it wasn't a thing. It was a drawing, a scribble of lines on the page. It wasn't even a proper drawing, not like Mrs Bolt told them to do in class, when she put down a vase of wilted flowers and said: *Draw what you see.* No, this was the kind of thing Enna did in the margins when she was restless, when her fingers wanted to be doing something else. It was doodling. Teachers told you off for it.

Enna often got restless. Most of life just seemed to move too slowly. So she doodled—faces, mostly. When she was happy the faces would be round and smiley; they would be jagged and snaggly when she was fed up. Today she'd been really fed up—it had been that sort of day from the beginning: grumpy breakfast, boring school, and everybody scratchy when she got home, so she'd come straight upstairs and shut the door behind her. She'd

1

sat staring at the open notebook. No way was she going to write Mrs Bolt a nice little poem about being an endangered species in the rainforest. She picked up a really sharp hard pencil and scribbled, almost hard enough to rip the pages. She did it with her eyes screwed up so tight that all she could see was an eyelashy blur . . . then she looked down to inspect what she'd done.

It was the snaggliest face ever, with a straggly beard, a hooked down nose, and big teeth bared in a nasty know-all sort of grin. It had a hand, where it rested its chin as if it was thinking—thinking wicked, snaggly, vicious, angry thoughts—and she drew the hand an arm, and drew the arm a shoulder, so you could tell it was squatting, with its back hunched. She knew what it looked like now: a gargoyle, one of those carvings they'd seen looking down on them from that cathedral in France last year. Enna remembered that: when Connie, all snotty and getting into being just-teenaged, turned to her and said in a voice loud enough for half of France to hear: *Oh, Enna, look, it's just like you.*

And the gargoyle on the page . . . Impossible, but it had moved.

The first time she looked it was in profile, sideways on. That's how she usually did her fierce ones, so she could make the nose really knobbly and the chin really long. Now that she looked again she thought . . . she felt . . . she could almost have sworn that it had turned its head a little, so she could see *both* its eyes. They were deep-set, dark with scribble, under those brambly eyebrows, so she couldn't quite see them, but she knew they would have heavy lids which never opened wide. Through the slits, though, it was peering at her.

Then it winked.

Enna shrieked and threw the notebook on the floor. It landed open—cover side upwards, luckily—and she picked it up at arm's length, as if it was hot. Taking care not to look she shut it and ran to the toy chest, dropped it in, and slammed the lid. She threw the bedspread over the chest, so she could not see it. Then she backed away.

Enna went downstairs. Already, halfway there, she could hear Mum and Wes down in the kitchen deep in conversation. She couldn't catch what they were saying, but it sounded serious.

It had been like this all day. OK, breakfast was never the sweetness-and-light time they'd have you believe on the cornflake packets. Mum would always be shouting upstairs: *Connie? Enna? Wake up Henry, will you? And I want you downstairs NOW!* But that's just family, thought Enna. Me and Connie have to wind each other up, till Mum says, *Stop it, both of you!* This morning, though, had been different. Mum was dressed in the kind of clothes you never, never saw her wear—plain and dark, sort of straight up and down, with a proper skirt, like, well . . . a business woman. Worse, she was nagging at Wes. When he appeared downstairs—moving kind of slow, in the cool way Wes did, just doing it faster than usual— Enna gasped. Wes was wearing a tie. Actually, he looked great, with jacket, shirt, and tie all toned just right for his coffee-cream complexion and his beard trimmed to a neat point. He looked a star. He just didn't look like the Wes Enna had grown to love ever since he'd been the big thing in Mum's life. And this morning he looked worried, too. There were no easy grins that morning, the kind of Wes grin that told Enna life was OK and Mum didn't mean it when she scolded. Nobody talked much over breakfast, and the three children were hustled out schoolwards, wondering what had hit them.

When Enna got back from school, nothing seemed better. She'd had to walk Henry home—that was another thing: Mum couldn't be there to fetch him, and he *was* only seven, and she *was* his sister, and . . . Enna had tuned out for the rest of what Mum said. But she'd brought Henry home. It was true, he was a spoiled little brat and a pain in the elbow, but she *was* his sister. Another day, it might even have been sweet, the way he rattled off everything he'd done today, and what the teacher had said, and . . .

'Oh, not now, Henry!' Enna had burst out, a bit like Mum did sometimes. Henry's eyes went wide for a moment, then he stumped on, being quiet. He just kept walking off pavements and dragging his bag and staring into people's windows, all the way home.

When they walked in, Mum wasn't in the café. No one was there, in fact, except old Mrs Grobowski, and she hardly counted as a customer. She came in and sat in silence, with one small black coffee, sometimes all day. Now she nodded to Enna. Mrs Grobowski never smiled, exactly, but there was a kind of mournful twinkle in her eye.

Mum and Wes were at the kitchen table, still talking. They looked worse than they had at breakfast, and they hardly said hello. Even Henry saw it would be a good idea to scuttle upstairs quietly. So did Enna, though there was a note from school about a trip, which Mrs Bolt had said she must give to her parents *right away*.

Don't stamp on the stairs, Mum called after her. *And do your homework*.

Yes, that was the kind of day it had been—one that called for a really scribbly angry face. But scribbles were meant to stay put, where you left them. They weren't meant to catch your eye, like a dirty old man, and wink. It was the wink that sent her downstairs, in a hurry, now.

'Mum . . . ?' said Enna as she came into the kitchen. Mum looked up, trying not to be impatient, then she saw the look on Enna's face. 'Something . . . happened. Something scary,' Enna said.

'What, love?'

'Well, I was drawing, and I drew this face, and it went all horrible, and . . . and then it winked at me.'

Mum's kind look suddenly went wooden. 'Oh, Enna, don't be silly,' she said. 'Can't you see there's something *important* going on?'

That was it. It must be one of those crises—probably Connie again. You'd think that being oldest, being fourteen, would mean you'd be better at things, but Connie managed to stage a crisis once or twice a week. 'Is it Connie again?' Enna said.

Wes kind of smiled and shook his head. 'Sorry, sugar,' he said. 'Things are a bit tense, that's all. We'll explain later. We got things we need to talk through first, you see?'

But by the time bedtime came, nobody had explained a thing. Enna lay in the bed trying to work it out. Mum came up to tuck her in. 'Mum?' said Enna. 'Are you and Wes . . . are you splitting up, like Gaynor's mum and dad?'

Mum looked at her, surprised, then gave a tired smile. 'No, no . . . Oh, sorry, love. Don't worry. It's nothing like that.' And she gave her a kiss and took the bedspread from the toy chest and tucked it in around the duvet, very snug and neat.

Enna lay there, in the half-light. There was a streetlight just outside and the curtains didn't quite reach to the edge of the window, so there was always a thin line of light that came in. Enna liked it. Tonight, though, it seemed to point across the carpet, to the toy chest in the corner of the room. Enna couldn't stop glancing at it. Mum had moved the bedspread, but the chest was solid enough. The heavy lid was tightly shut. The trouble was, Enna knew what was inside it.

The notebook. The face. That snaggly beard, those overhanging eyebrows and those deep-set eyes . . . In her mind's eye she could see it, as clear as she'd seen it on the page . . . except that it had moved a bit more, turning round to face her, and the grin was getting wider all the time.

It was trapped. She'd slammed the lid on it. How would she feel if she'd been shut in there? Angry, that's how. Enna shuddered. What would happen next time someone raised the lid?

6

How was Enna meant to get to sleep, with that in there? She tried. She tried. She couldn't.

Then after a while she thought: it only winked at me. What if it was trying to be friendly? What if it couldn't help the way it looked? *She'd* drawn it that way, after all. Then she'd thrown it away. How would *she* feel, if she'd smiled at someone and they bunged her in a trunk and locked her in? Wouldn't she feel sad, as well as angry?

Enna looked at the chest and she could almost see those scribbly eyes down in the darkness of it, looking sideways at the tiny crack of light. What if it was just sad. Left out? *Lonely?*

Enna wasn't going to get a wink of sleep tonight, unless . . . Unless . . . She had to have a look.

Chapter 2

Draw Me In

Enna opened the lid . . . very slowly,
just a crack . . . then a little bit more,
till the light from the window fell into
the chest and she could see.

Nothing there. It was just a toy chest,
full of things she didn't use much any
more. Her old dressing-up clothes were tangled up
together, and there was the tatty pink feather boa old
Maggie Aspidistra gave her years and years ago. There
was a neat small heap of all those Beanie Babies she'd
badgered Mum for, till she gave in with a sigh. Money
was tight, what with the café having problems, and Enna
had pretended to go on playing with them long after
the rest of the class lost interest in theirs, just for Mum's
sake. Then there were old magazines and school books
and all the stuff she'd flung in there some time when
Mum would call: *I'm coming up in five minutes and if that
bedroom isn't tidy* . . .

And there was the notebook, with its stripy cover.
She hadn't seen it at first, but there it was, slipped down
the side, behind the feather boa. Enna took a deep
breath and picked it up. She laid it flat on the floor, in
the light from the window. Now, she had to look.

It fell open on the page, and the gargoyle face was
looking straight up, as if it was expecting her.

Its lips moved. 'Hhhuhhmuhhh,' it said.

Enna stared. For it to move a bit, that's one thing.

8

But to *speak* . . . ? That's just silly. Impossible. Then it did it again. It was a small voice, thin and papery, and sort of muffled. She leaned closer. 'Help me,' it said.

It was struggling; she could see that. All its lines were bending, stretching, like something caught in a trap. 'Help me!' It didn't sound angry—more like desperate.

'How?' whispered Enna.

'Draw me in. Finish me.'

Enna fumbled with her pencil case. Pencils, felt pens, and pretty rubbers spilled out on the carpet, but she left them there. This was an emergency; she could feel it. The pencil wobbled in her grip as she brought it towards the paper. Her hand felt big and clumsy. What was she meant to do next?

The thing on the page was nothing but a head and arms and shoulders. It looked as if it had pushed its top part through the paper from the other side, and got stuck halfway.

'H-how?' said Enna. 'I don't know what you look like.'

'Look me in the eye.' As she did, she got the feeling. It might have been a memory, from that cathedral they'd visited in Paris, but she could see the figure crouching, with shaggy hind legs crooked up beneath it, and on its hunched back there were rather elegantly folded bat-like wings.

'Now,' it said. 'Draw!'

'I can't draw.'

The thing just sighed. If it had had hips it would have put its hands on them, like Mum did when she was losing her patience. 'You drew me this far. What kind of scribe are you?'

'Scribe? All I can do is doodle.'

'Well, *do dull* some more.' Its voice was shrill now. 'It's true. You don't know what you're doing, do you?'

'No! You tell me.' They stared at each other. 'I was just . . . I don't know. I was angry. Fed up.'

'Good!' the thing said. 'Remember that.' She screwed her eyes tight again. There'd been Mum being snappy over breakfast, and Miss Crop-top Connie looking down her nose at her, and Henry being a pain—all the usual—and . . . And suddenly the pencil tip was moving. 'Yes!' she heard the creature whisper. 'Don't stop. That's it . . . Yes!'

Enna didn't dare look. 'Thank you,' the voice said, soft as paper rustling in the wind. Enna opened her eyes.

She could have cried with disappointment. Yes, there was the picture, more or less the way she'd seen it in her head. But it was only a picture. Its head was in profile, the way it had been when she had drawn it first, and it was motionless. It felt empty. No one at home.

'Wonderful,' said the small voice. '*Mirabilis*.' Enna looked up. It hadn't come from the drawing but there, on the edge of the light, perched on the side of the toy chest, was the squatting thing. It was real, and alive, and it was touching itself all over—arms, legs, feet—as if it couldn't quite believe that it was there. 'Yes!' it said. 'Yes! *Real!*' The strangest thing was that it was still an outline—like a cartoon, a pale line in the air with dark inside it. 'Thank you,' it said again.

'Who . . . I mean, what are you?'

It got to its feet—a little stiffly—and turned to the right, and to the left, and bowed towards her gravely. Then suddenly it flexed and turned a cartwheel off the chest. As it came upright on the carpet, full in the light now, its scraggly beard split open in a toothy grin.

'Don't be afraid,' it said. 'It's always a shock, the first time. Would it help if I was bigger?'

'No . . . ! I mean: *how much* bigger . . . ?'

'That varies.' It shrugged. 'It's just a matter of perspective,' it added, mysteriously, and with a little shiver and a shake its outline rippled outwards to double the size.

'That's enough,' said Enna, quickly.

'As you wish.' It stretched its arms and yawned. It shook its legs, one by one, stamped whatever it had for feet, then gave a frisk all over like a wet dog. Finally, it uncrumpled its wings. They weren't big but they spread out taut and glossy as a sailboard's sails. Enna gasped as they rippled with watery patterns, like Wes's brown silk shirt held up to the light. There was detail in it drawn in by a point almost too fine for the human eye to see.

The thing folded its wings back round it like a cosy little cape.

'Who are you?' Enna said. 'What's your name?'

'Name? We don't need them, really, *out there*. We're called . . . whatever you like. What would you like to call me?'

'This is a dream,' said Enna, closing her eyes. 'When I open my eyes you won't be there.'

11

'Why are you still talking to me, then?' the voice came. 'What was that word you used? *Do dull?*'

'Doodle.'

'Very well,' it said perkily. 'You want a name? You can call me the Dood.' She opened her eyes. She couldn't help it; he sounded so pleased with himself. And she had to admit, it wasn't *it* but *he*. Now she looked, the Dood began to laugh. 'That was meant to be a joke,' he said. 'But I like it.' And he did a little caper, clapped his hands to his stomach, doubled over, with his wings wrapped round him, chortling like a silly kid.

'Hold it right there.' If there was one thing Enna didn't like, it was people having private jokes. Connie and her gang seemed to do it all the time, giggling together in that way you had to notice. 'If you've just stepped out of nowhere, how come you speak English?'

'Hmmm . . . Complicated. I came through your head, like I came through your writing stick.'

'So . . . you know what I'm thinking?'

'Not exactly. You don't know everything your mother thinks, do you?'

'You mean I'm, like . . . your mother. Yuck!'

'What's so *yuck* about it?'

'For one thing, you're *old*. And for another . . . ' Enna caught herself in mid breath. What was she doing, arguing with someone who didn't exist? 'I'm fed up with this. If I thought you up, I can unthink you. You can just go back right now.'

He didn't move. 'But there must be a reason,' he said. 'I wouldn't *be* here if—Hey!'

12

Enna had taken a swipe at him. 'Shoo!' she said. 'Vanish!'

'Wait!' his voice said, just behind her shoulder. 'This is a historic moment. You should—' She wheeled round and grabbed, but he was gone.

'—be honoured,' said the voice, from somewhere else. 'We have so much to *say* to each other.'

Enna reached for the light switch and, just for a moment, blinking at the dazzle, she caught a glimpse of him, crouching in the shelter of the chest. She plunged her hands in, rooting round, then paused. He was cornered. All she had to do was take things out one at a time. She shook each magazine, each bit of fabric, just in case, but he didn't drop out. He must be in the bottom, cowering. She lifted out the last thing. And he wasn't there.

In the bottom of the chest, though, was a crack *so* thin—a paper's width, no more.

'I know more about you than you think . . . '

The voice came from over by the wardrobe. He was in the corner, shrunk back down to doodle size. Enna didn't stop to think, but grabbed again. This time he didn't leap away. Quite what happened, she couldn't have said. It might be that she didn't dare to touch— that she flinched at the very last moment, like when she tried to pick up a live frog for the first time. Either that, or he slipped between her fingers—yes, *between* them. From the corner of her eye, she caught a movement by the bed . . .

'Outside . . . Left out . . . even when you're in the middle,' he squeaked. 'You know what that's like, don't you? Mark my words!'

13

That was the last straw. It was *so* annoying, the smug way old people say that. No way was she going to *Mark my words*. He must have seen the look on her face, the way he flattened himself against the wallpaper; for a moment he looked just like a small kid's scribble. Enna cupped her hands flat on the wall and tried to scoop him, but the lines just wriggled and were gone. It was hopeless. Every time she looked, he wasn't there. Then a sharp little sound behind her—a rip, like paper—made her turn.

In the scatter of things from the toy chest there was one slight movement. The notebook still lay open and the movement was the ragged edge of a page. The page where the doodle had been. She picked it up. Yes, it was torn out, not very neatly, and she didn't have to ask who by. Her drawing was the way the Dood had come through from—what did he say: *the other side*? It was like his doorway. Now he'd run off and taken it with him, and she couldn't shut it any more.

Chapter 3

Sorry Street

Some time in the small hours, Enna fell asleep. Some things are just too strange to think about. The trouble is, you can't stop trying . . .

The next thing she knew it was morning. She looked at the clock—past nine: she'd slept in. Thank heavens it wasn't a school day, or Mum would have been banging on the door at half past seven. Worse, she'd have burst in, and seen . . . The room looked as if a bomb had gone off. The toy chest lay upended on the floor, along with things hauled out of the cupboard as she'd hunted in the middle of the night.

It all came back. There on the floor was the notebook. Enna fumbled through it. Please, she thought, let it have been a dream.

If it had been a dream, she'd find her doodle, still there. But she didn't. If it hadn't, she would find a page torn out. She did.

She sat down. Take a deep breath, she thought. Work it out. There had to be an explanation. Then she thought of a programme they'd watched about sleepwalkers— how they would wake up downstairs in the kitchen, making breakfast in the middle of the night. Well, if people can boil an egg in their sleep, maybe they can tear up notebooks and not remember in the morning? And as for the—*what* did it call itself?—the Dood . . . She closed her eyes and the outline of him flickered in her mind, and winked. No! The thing had been a dream, and that was that.

Downstairs, breakfast had been and gone. There were sounds of a computer game coming from the sitting room—Henry kind of sounds. In the kitchen she met Connie, looking tousled in her dressing gown. This was normal for Saturday. Connie wouldn't appear until midday, looking spruced and made-up and just rushing out to meet her friends in town. This was an early morning coffee raid, and it was never a good idea to get in the way of Connie, then.

'Shut the door!' hissed Connie. 'Oh my God, what if they bring him upstairs? He might see me like this!'

'Who?' said Enna.

'Don't you ever notice what's going on? Him, downstairs, with Mum and Wes. He looks about eighteen, but I looked out of the window and he's got a BMW.'

'Who?' said Enna again.

'The estate agent.' Connie caught hold of Enna by both shoulders. 'It's going to happen at last. We're going to get out of this crummy old backstreet. We'll go and live somewhere proper. Somewhere I can bring my friends home.'

'What's wrong with here? I like Surrey Street.'

'Sorry Street! That's what everybody calls it . . . in case you didn't know.'

'Moving . . . ?' Enna frowned. 'You mean they're selling the café?'

'Yes! Isn't that brilliant?'

'But . . . Mum's worked really hard. She doesn't want to leave, I know she doesn't.'

'She'll get over it. I mean, who comes in here except old hippies and grannies. Really, it's like a day-centre for sad people. It's *embarrassing*.' Connie dropped her hands from Enna's shoulders. 'Oh,' she said, 'when you're my age you'll understand.'

Enna dragged her feet along the pavement. Yes, Sorry Street: she knew people called it that. She did feel sorry for it, looking at the windows that would have been shops until they closed down. Some had metal shutters up; some just had boards, with flyposters all over them, several layers deep. Some had signs up, TO LET, but they'd been like that as long as Enna could remember. People left. Only last year Gaynor, one of Enna's best friends in her class at school, had moved with her mum and sister, somewhere on the edge of town. She'd sent a card at Christmas saying how it was all wide open and empty out there and she missed Surrey Street.

Still, people left and no one seemed to want to move in, except the squatters in number 34. Enna remembered when the wool shop went, then the butcher's. There was still the clothes shop but it had a left-behind feeling, like the Aspidistra sisters who ran it. They weren't really called that, but Wes had said it once, not unkindly, and it stuck. *Old hippies and grannies*, Connie had said: the Aspidistras still wore flowery things or faded velvet. They had a window full of heaps of velvet, tie-dye, PVC, and antique lace—more like a hamster nest than a shop. They couldn't be making much money, because one of them, Jenny, helped out in the café too sometimes. She

17

was quite sweet really. They weren't sisters, either, and the plant in their window wasn't an aspidistra but a tatty cheese-plant, and so that was that.

Besides, it was Maggie Aspidistra who gave Enna the old feather boa. Who'd do things like that if they left Surrey Street?

Now it was only really the Siderious' corner shop which was doing OK but only, Mum said, because they kept the whole family working their hind legs off day and night, even Nico, who was Enna's age. Enna thought Nico might be OK, even if his family did send him to a private school. He never wore his posh blazer as if he really meant it, and you'd see him at the end of the road swinging it on his finger; then he'd slip it on quickly as he came in sight of home. Enna and Nico weren't on chatting terms, exactly, but they kind of smiled when they passed each other in the street.

'Hey, princess!' boomed a voice from inside the shop. There was old Mr Sideriou. 'Why the long face on a sunny day?'

Enna gave him a smile—she couldn't help it. Mr Sideriou was grand. He had a glossy moustache and opened up his corner shop each morning, Mum said, as if it was an *emporium*. 'Good, good. Hey, Nico, give the girl a mango. No!' He raised a hand. 'No charge. Can't sell them—but hey, just mind the black bits and they're *sweet*.'

Nico came out with two. In a sloppy grey sweatshirt he looked like . . . well, someone who works in a shop, not a boy from St Catherine's. He gave her a shy sidelong grin.

'Thanks,' Enna said. 'Mum says you should always wash fruit first . . . '

'Better eat it here, then,' said Nico. 'She'll never know.' There was something in the way he said it that made her smile, and then they were smiling together, her and Nico and old Mr Sideriou. There was a *ding!* from the shop and Nico's uncle vanished back inside.

'Embarrassing, isn't he?' said Nico.

'No, he's nice!'

'Ah . . . ' Nico screwed up his face. 'But imagine it *every day*. Think of it *over breakfast*! Now, your parents, they look nice.'

'Oh, please!' said Enna.

'OK, OK, truce! You know what to do with a mango? No, you need a knife. Come round the back and I'll show you the trick. Come on—family-free zone.'

'Are we allowed to? I mean, aren't you meant to be helping in the shop?'

'No problem. Uncle, he's a big softie. It's Grandma you've got to watch out for. Coming?'

'OK.'

They ducked down the alley marked Private, past the overflowing wheelie bins and into the little back yard. It was piled with empty boxes, plus a row of flowerpots with trailing creepers reaching for the sun. There was a squat dog on a chain, who bared his teeth. 'Don't mind Aristotle,' Nico said. 'He's a softie too.' He reached out a hand and Aristotle licked it. Enna offered hers, too.

'People are usually scared of him,' said Nico. 'Specially girls . . . You're not much like a girl.'

19

'Thanks!'

'Sorry. I mean . . . not a girly sort of girl. Not like my sisters.'

'Mine too,' Enna said. 'Well then, what's the trick?'

'You watch.' Nico ducked inside the back door and came back with a slightly scary kitchen knife. 'First,' he said, 'lay the patient on the operating table.' He balanced the mango on a packing case. 'Nurse? Scalpel . . . '

'You going to be a doctor, then?'

'That's what my family tells me. Grandma decided. Now . . . ' With two quick snicks of the knife he sliced the mango, end to end—two nearly-halves, leaving just a sliver with the flat stone in it in the middle. 'This is the magic bit . . . ' With the tip of the knife he scored a this-way-that-way pattern in the orange flesh, then picked up a piece and flipped it inside out. Perfect cubes of ripe flesh stood up, peeling themselves off the inside of the skin. 'Enjoy!' Five minutes later, Enna was still licking the sticky-slippery juice from her fingers. 'Uncle was right, though,' Nico, said. 'You looked really fed up, out there.'

'What would you do,' said Enna, 'if your family told you you were moving?'

Nico looked up sharply. 'You aren't, are you?'

'Don't know. Nobody's saying much. But something's going on.'

'Sounds like my family all the time,' said Nico.

'And this estate agent came round . . . '

'That sounds bad.' Nico frowned, thinking. 'If mine told me we were moving . . . I'd run away.'

'If you ran away, you'd still be moving.'

'Hmmm. Then I'd wait until they moved and then I'd run back here.' Suddenly the two were laughing. Just like friends, thought Enna. And why not, after all?

'Come on,' said Nico. 'D'you want to come along the Edge?'

'Edge?' She looked where he was pointing.

Behind this side of Surrey Street, you didn't get a garden. The ground went up a step, towards the High Street. There was a wall in some places, red sandy rock in others and a lot of ivy trailing down. When you looked out of Connie's window, upstairs at the back, you could just see the rear ends of parked cars in the office car park. 'Carbon monoxide!' Connie had said dramatically one morning over breakfast. 'It's stunting my growth. If it wasn't for that . . . '

'You'd be Naomi Campbell, yeah,' Enna had said, as Connie grabbed at her.

'Stop it, you two,' Mum had said. 'You're both nearly as tall as me already.'

It wasn't a beautiful prospect, the back yards of Surrey Street. But the Edge, now . . . that looked promising. Halfway up the bulgy sandstone, higher than their heads, was a kind of fault line, where the rock was crumbly, washed away by years of rain. By the wall of the yard, it widened to a ledge that you could crouch on, if you went on hands and knees. You could even creep behind the ivy . . . Enna looked at Nico with a new respect.

'Or would you rather go on looking miserable?' said Nico.

'Are you allowed?' said Enna.

'Course not. But most of the houses are empty. Coming? Quiet, Aristotle, boy.'

'Do you know?' Enna said as she scrambled onto the wall beside Nico. 'I used to think you were posh.'

'Do you know?' Nico said. 'My grandma says they send me to St Catherine's so I won't have to mix with kids like you.'

'Me? Huh! I'm the sensible one, in my family.'

'Poor you,' Nico said. 'Sensible? Really?'

'You should see the rest of them!' There was a pause as they picked their way over a strand of barbed wire. 'What if we're caught?'

'No problem,' said Nico. 'It'll be your fault. Besides, this place is secret. No families, no nagging, no bother. How about that?'

'You bet,' said Enna.

'Follow me.'

Chapter 4

The Stone Age

The ledge beneath her hands and knees was gritty but not wet. It would brush off, Enna reckoned, so Mum wouldn't take one look at her and say *Enna? Where've you been?* She didn't want Mum to ask because she wouldn't want to tell her, and it made her feel sort of sick inside to tell a bare-faced lie.

It was the cobwebs that bothered her. This was Spider City. As she pushed through the tunnel of ivy behind Nico she could feel the cobwebs snagging in her hair. Something tickled down the back of her neck. She shuddered.

Nico was looking back, grinning. But she wasn't going to go all squealy and girlish—not while he was watching. With another wriggle Enna pushed through and came out with him. 'Here we are,' he said.

It wasn't a cave, exactly—just a higher, deeper bit of ledge—but here the ivy hung free like a curtain, just letting in speckles of light. It was like the secret space behind a waterfall. There was space for them to sit, with their knees up to their faces. Nico parted the ivy curtain and they peered out, like spies.

From the back, Surrey Street looked different. Of course she'd seen her own house from the back yard, but from here . . . It was like looking in on all this through a peep-hole from another time, another world. They could be in the Stone Age.

'See?' Nico took a deep breath. 'Good, eh?'

23

'Sort of sad, too,' Enna said. 'It all looks . . . so empty. Everybody's leaving. Doesn't it worry you?'

'It worries Uncle. *That's our business going*, he says.' Nico shrugged. 'They're all worriers, my family. You should see them at the dinner table. Like an Olympic worrying team. What good does it do?' There was a pause.

'You can always come here,' he said cautiously, 'if it gets bad at home.'

'I wish I could *live* here,' said Enna. 'I mean, when the others move away. Think of it—no more Connie, no more Henry!'

'What's so wrong with them?'

'Oh, nothing!' Enna gave a snort. 'Only that Connie gets to lie in bed till lunchtime, *and* gets out of doing her chores, *and* barricades herself into the bathroom—the only bathroom, with the loo in—for an hour!' And whatever it was she did in there, Enna thought, it didn't make her any happier; she always came downstairs in a bad mood. She never understood why people thought Connie was pretty—as if all the eyeliner and lipstick in the world could cover up that scowl.

'Sisters!' Nico laughed. 'She's just going through a stage.'

'You sound like Jenny Aspidistra. I heard her and Mum in the café. *Sometimes I just can't bring myself to ask her if she's tidied her room* . . . Mum said it herself. *It's just not worth the battle.* And you know what Jenny said to her?'

They chimed together: '*She's just going through a stage.*'

'And then there's Henry. Mister Cute himself. You should see the old ladies in the café fussing round him.

24

Then there's me . . . Can you be *left out in the middle*?'
For a moment Enna had a funny feeling. The words had
popped out of her mouth. Where had she heard them
before? Nico gave her a wry smile.

'Chance would be a fine thing. If you had a family
like mine, you'd *dream* of being left out! Why do you
think I come here?'

'To be a caveman?'

He looked at her a moment, puzzled. Then he
grinned. 'Yeah!' He stuck his lips out, ape-style.

'We could lie in wait for prey here . . . ' Enna said.

'Dinosaurs!'

'No, mammoths. And when one comes we swing
down on the creepers . . . '

' . . . and chop!' He did a little Tarzan imitation.
'Then we make a fire.'

'How?'

'Two stones. Or something. Then we dance around
it, and we do a human sacrifice.'

'I don't think they did that,' said Enna. 'We did the
Stone Age at school, and Mrs Bolt said . . . '

'Not history,' said Nico, 'please! You want to talk
about history, you talk to Grandma. They go on about
it all the time. Come on, forget the mammoths. Let's
explore.'

They edged along a little further, till the ivy got too
dense. There were stems of it, all twisted round each
other, as thick as Jack's beanstalk. Nico swung out on
one of them and shinned down into the yard, as if he
owned it.

'Careful!' Enna said. 'Someone might . . . '

25

'No chance. No one's been here for years. Come on, look for yourself.'

Enna came up behind him, cautiously. A few windows overlooked the yard but they all had a blank look. Inside the back window, where a dining room should be, she saw bare floorboards, some of them ripped up. Through the gap, tangled wires stuck up in the air. Enna pressed her nose against the frosted glass of the back door. Then she sniffed.

'Nico?' she said. 'Do you smoke?'

'Yuck! Mug's game. You don't, do you?'

'No, but someone does.' Nico looked where Enna's toe was pointing. On the doorstep were the little thin ends of someone's smokes—the home-made kind, but in brown paper—several of them, all bent at right-angles, as if someone half smoked them then got fed up and stubbed them out quite hard. 'I thought you said no one came here,' Enna said.

They looked at each other. Suddenly the empty house felt not so empty. 'Uh . . . I think we should go now,' said Nico, and they did.

As they climbed down into the Siderious' yard, Enna hung back. She didn't quite know how to say the next bit. 'Nico . . . if . . . just imagine you were looking at a picture in a book, and it spoke to you, what would you do?'

'Is this a video or something?'

'No, no. What if it was . . . real?'

Nico gave her a look. 'Then I'd think you had a kind of weird imagination.'

'But if it was *you*, and it did, and . . . '

'I'd keep quiet about it. Go round saying things like

26

that and they'll have you sent away!' Suddenly he grinned and snapped his fingers. 'You think too much! Now, no more talking pictures. This is more fun, isn't it?' And Enna could hardly say No.

She was out in the street and halfway home when there was a kerfuffle: car horns and the rev of engines. A lorry was trying to squeeze its way past a parked car. Or no, the car wasn't parked but dumped, in the middle of the narrow road. They'd had a lot of that lately. Usually the windows were broken and things ripped out. Joyriding was what people called it, but there didn't seem much joy in it to Enna. Poor old Surrey Street. But she loved it—even if it was a bit sad. She wasn't going to let them move her, just like that.

The house felt tense when she walked in. Mum and Wes were standing by the window. They looked pale and strange. 'What is it?' said Enna. Surely she hadn't been out as long as that?

'Sit down,' said Mum. 'We meant to have a talk with you last night, but . . . ' She trailed off.

'We're moving, aren't we?'

'Moving? Hah!' It was like a laugh, but she could see it wasn't funny. Enna had never heard Wes sound like that before. *Easy, easy,* that was his way. Mum was the one who got ruffled; Wes would wait a while, then say, *Easy, let's sit down and talk this through* . . . Then he caught Enna's eye. 'Oh, sorry, sweetheart. We'd better start from the beginning. You see, we saw the bank manager yesterday . . . '

27

'And he sat us down and said we weren't to take it personally . . . ' Mum said, 'but what with Surrey Street not being *a sought-after area* . . . The very opposite in fact. What with it *going downhill* . . . He didn't think the café was *a sound investment.*'

'In other words,' Wes cut in, 'the bank wants their money back. Pronto.'

'We don't have that kind of money,' Mum said. 'Not unless we sell up.'

'So Connie was right,' said Enna. 'She said we were moving.'

Wes gave that bitter little laugh again. 'If only!' he said. 'Then this estate agent kid, this public school smoothie, comes round and tells us how much we could sell it for. Peanuts. No one wants a place like this.'

'Why?' Enna said.

'Because it's Surrey Street, that's why.'

Mum looked very serious. 'The thing is,' she said, 'with the money we'd get . . . we couldn't start another café. It would be like giving it away. After all our hard work.'

Enna looked at them. 'So . . . what are we going to do?'

There was a silence that scared Enna more than anything she'd heard so far. 'Leave it to your mum and me,' said Wes. 'We'll figure something out. You're not to worry.'

'But . . . '

'Just give us a while to mull it over,' Mum said and gave her a quick hug. 'I think you'd better go and make sure Henry's OK.' Enna bit her lip. As she got up to go, she glanced towards Wes, who had turned to run hot water in the sink. As the steam rose, misting up the window, Enna saw a shape, a faint squiggly outline reappearing like something someone had drawn there in the steam before. Enna gasped. With Nico, half an hour ago, she'd almost made her mind up: she wouldn't brood on things—no more talking pictures. But look, there it was, and it wasn't her imagination. No one had seen the Dood but her. But someone—or something—had left its likeness, like a signature, on the glass.

'Mum . . . ?'

'Can it wait, love? Now really isn't the moment . . .'

Enna looked at Mum and Wes, but their hands were busy with the washing up, and their minds were miles away. *Outside . . . left out . . . even when you're in the middle . . .* Enna found herself thinking. *You know what that's like, don't you? Mark my words . . .* And she had, she did.

Chapter 5

Imaginary Friends

Henry crouched at the computer with his back to her, zapping aliens with his joystick. Each one he hit (and she had to admit, his score was getting quite impressive) vanished with a little splat of cartoon blood. For a moment Enna imagined one of the zap-things ricocheting back out of the screen and splat! Henry would vanish, just like that.

She blinked. She didn't hate him really. From behind, she could see why old ladies just had to walk up and ruffle his hair, and say things like *Bless his cotton socks*. But he was in his own world, and he hadn't even glanced at her.

'Henry?'

'Wait a minute. It's coming . . . Wow!' One of the aliens loomed towards them, a kind of flailing octopus shape, filling half the screen. Henry loosed a salvo at it, ripping off four or five limbs. 'Wicked!' Henry whooped. 'Oh, no . . . ' As they watched (and Enna was watching too; she couldn't help it) the blasted-off bits dissolved and formed into a clump and started to morph into something else with jaws and teeth and horns.

'What *is* it?' Enna said.

'Shapeshifter 3,' said Henry. 'Brilliant . . . '

'Henry . . . ' she said again. But he was locked in mortal combat. Enna turned back to the door.

Maybe Henry was going through a

30

stage, she thought—like Connie, only his stage was called Being Cute.

She needed to talk to her mum. The Dood's face, that ugly mug, was real, scribbled on the kitchen window. She couldn't get it out of her mind. She closed her eyes but it just became clearer. It was all very well for Wes to say, *You're not to worry*. He didn't know there was a wild thing, a gargoyle with attitude, loose in the house.

Enna peeped in through the crack in the kitchen door. Mum was alone now, standing by the window, a dishcloth in hand, and the Dood's face was gone.

'Mum?' said Enna faintly. 'Can I talk to you?'

'Oh, Enna,' Mum said. 'I'm sorry if it worried you, that stuff about the bank. Maybe we said too much.'

'It's not that. Remember what I told you yesterday?'

'Yesterday?' Mum's face was blank. 'I'm sorry, love. We've got so much on our minds . . . '

'The drawing . . . ' Enna said. 'The one that winked at me . . . '

Mum sat down, rather stiffly, and sat Enna on her knee. 'Now,' she said, 'I know all this is hard for you. I know I've been hassled, and I've probably been a bit preoccupied. But . . . it wasn't the right moment for a game.'

'It's not a game, Mum.'

'Enna, love, it is. You've got a good imagination . . . '

'No . . . !' Enna jumped up. 'It's escaped. I've seen it running round my bedroom. It's in the house somewhere, hiding . . . ' Mum was looking at her with a strange expression. Enna couldn't stop. 'Didn't you see the picture on the window? It must have drawn it itself. Like a message, or . . . '

'Stop!' said Mum sharply. Then she hugged her. 'Enna, love, you mustn't. You're winding yourself up. The more you think about it, the more you'll start imagining things.'

Mum leaned back so Enna could look straight in her eyes. She was so close that Enna could see the flecks of brown in them, and the small specks of mascara where they'd fallen off her lashes.

'This is a bad time,' said Mum. 'I'm not surprised you need a bit of comfort. Lots of people have imaginary friends. I remember Nuggle—used to go everywhere with you, to playgroup, even in the bath . . . '

'Mum!' Enna yelped. 'It's not like Nuggle.'

Mum went on. 'All of us are getting stressed out, and it takes us different ways. Wes, now, he just goes off on his own and plays his music. Me, I clean a lot. I noticed Henry had his sucky cloth the other night . . . '

'But it's *real*.'

Enna wriggled out of Mum's hug. Wes had appeared in the doorway.

'Hey, girls . . . Enna, is your mum trying to psycho-analyse you?' He stroked his beard. 'Now . . . *ven did zees symptoms first appear* . . . ?'

Enna burst into tears. 'What did I say?' said Wes, as she ducked between them and ran out of the door.

Back in the sitting room, the computer game was over. As Enna wiped her eyes, Henry looked up. There was a smile on his face that could have made her *really* angry, but . . .

'I drew it,' he said.

'What?'

'Your magic picture. *It must have drawn it itself . . .* ' he mimicked.

'Hey, you were listening, weren't you? You dirty little earwigger!'

Henry ducked out of her way. 'I only heard bits,' he said. 'You were mumbling. Mum thinks you're going nuts.'

She grabbed at him . . . then stopped as if she'd hit a glass wall. 'Just a minute. You drew it? Honestly?'

'Yes.'

'Then . . . Then you've seen it.'

'Course I have.'

'*Tell* her, then. Tell her you've seen it. Tell her I'm not crazy.' Enna paused. Henry was eying her with his junior chess-master look. 'OK,' she said. 'What do you want?'

'A bumper pack of football stickers. No, three . . . Ouch!' he said as Enna pinned him to the ground. 'I'll shout!'

'Tell Mum you've seen it,' said Enna. 'Henry, please! Tell her it's real.' A pause. 'OK,' she said, 'you can have your stickers.'

Henry smiled. 'You sure you want me to? She'll take it away.'

'What do you mean: take it away? She'll never catch it.'

'Catch it?' Henry said. 'You *are* nuts. It's just a bit of paper.'

Enna let go of him, fast. 'Hang on,' she said. 'You found the drawing?'

'Down behind my radiator. I didn't know it was special. I just thought it had a funny face.'

'And you haven't seen . . . *it*.' He was staring at her. OK, let him think she'd gone mad. She wished she hadn't said that, but she couldn't back out now. And Henry was starting to look interested.

'Will you let me see . . . *it*?' Their eyes met. This was the Henry Enna knew, if other people didn't. It puzzled Enna that nobody, not even Mum, saw that under that sweet baby-face there was a calculating brain at work, cool as a chess grand master, even if he did cry when he fell down in the street and grazed his knee. Once they got down to bargaining, she knew that there was no way she could win. 'Will you, if I tell you where the drawing is?'

'Yes. Tell me.'

'Do I get the stickers?'

'Yes, yes. Where's the drawing?'

'Stickers first,' said Henry. 'And you tell me all about . . . *it*. And . . . '

The list of demands could have got much longer, but he didn't reach the end of it. Downstairs, a door banged, and Mum gave a shriek, the way she did when she was very, very cross.

Chapter 6

Number Withheld

'How dare they?' Mum was shouting, as the children crept downstairs. 'How *dare* they?'

Wes was out on the pavement, staring up and down the street, as if some kids were playing Knockout Ginger. But Mum was standing there, trembling with anger, with a typewritten letter in her hand.

'What's wrong?' said Enna.

Wes came back inside. 'Someone's made us an offer.'

'Oh,' said Enna. 'Isn't that what you wanted?'

'Peanuts!' Mum said. 'And there isn't a name, or a number or anything. There's something about this I don't like at all. Look at the last line.' She thrust the letter into Wes's hands.

'*You would be well advised to respond without delay.* Just business language,' he said.

'Business language? It's a threat.' Mum took the letter back out of Wes's hands and ripped it up and threw the pieces in the bin. She did it with style. Mum could be sort of magnificent when she was angry, thought Enna—at least when she was angry with somebody else, not her.

A little later, Enna and Henry walked into the corner shop. 'A bumper pack of those things,' Enna muttered. 'No, make that three.'

Nico was there. He grinned at Enna. 'I didn't know you liked football,' he said.

'Not me. Him,' Enna said. Henry put on his cute face.

'Wow, my little brother doesn't get pocket money like that. Is it his birthday?'

'Yeah,' said Enna. 'Every day.' She glanced at Henry, ready for some smart-guy answer. But he was ripping packets open and shuffling his stickers, happy as any ordinary seven year old. For a moment Enna almost forgot this was a business deal and hugged him. Then she remembered. 'Come on,' she said, and she marched him home.

They had to wait till later in the afternoon before they knew they wouldn't be disturbed. Even so, Enna put a chair behind the door in Henry's room. 'Now,' she said.

As Henry pulled out the torn page from beneath his mattress Enna reached to take it, but he held it closer to his chest. 'OK,' said Enna. 'On the floor, between us. Nice and flat.'

And there it was—the Dood face, just the way she had drawn it. It was looking sideways with its old gnarled profile. In fact, Enna thought with a rush of annoyance, it seemed to be ignoring them. But no, it was only a drawing. It was empty, like the other night, when the Dood had come through it and left.

'Make it come,' said Henry.

Enna stared at the page. All she saw was a bored kid's scribble. It looked ugly, mean, and angry, and for a moment Enna thought: maybe that's just *me*, all mean and angry.

'Well?' said Henry.

Enna buried her face in her hands. 'It's not fair,' she

36

said. 'Not fair. I don't know how.' When she looked up, the drawing was gone. 'Put it back . . . '

'No deal,' said Henry. 'You said I could see *it*.'

Enna threw herself at Henry. As she got her fingers to the paper, he whispered, 'I'll call Mum.'

'Don't care.'

'You'll tear it,' he said. *Tear it?* Enna let go. What would happen if she did? What if the Dood was out here, in the house, in this world . . . and they tore up its picture like Mum had torn up the letter in the hall? What if the Dood lost its door to the other place, and could never get back? What then?

'All right, all right,' she said. 'Just watch that drawing. The Dood might come back. If not, we'll have to try again.'

The phone went in the middle of the night. It only ever did that when there was bad news, like when Grandad went into hospital. Enna sat up, her heart thumping, wide awake. She could hear Mum's voice in the hall.

'Hello?' Mum said. 'Who is that? Who am I talking to?' Then for a long while she said nothing, then there was a clunk. Mum slammed the phone down, and she hadn't even said Goodbye.

Seconds later, the phone rang again.

Wes was out there with Mum now, and Enna crept to the door. 'No!' Wes's voice was tight. She eased the door a little open. 'No,' he said again. 'The answer's no.'

'Quick,' Mum said as he put the phone down. 'Get

the number.' Wes was already punching the numbers in, the ones that tell you who's just called. 'Damn,' he said after a moment. 'Surprise, surprise. *The caller withheld their number.*'

Enna crept out on the landing. There was Connie, too, standing in the shadows, listening.

'What's going on?' said Enna.

'Don't know. I thought we were moving . . . '

'Something's wrong, isn't it? Connie, I'm scared.'

Connie was biting her lip. She looked younger than Enna had seen her for years, and didn't pull away when Enna slipped her hand in hers. 'They'll tell us in the morning,' she said, and gave Enna's hand a squeeze. 'Let's go back to bed.'

Creak. Enna sat up and looked at the clock. Half past six. Sometimes the postman made a noise, but not like this. It was a gritty grating sound, like something being dragged, outside in the street. Enna went to the window but the street was empty—except for the sound, right underneath the window, too close against the house to see. Kicking on her fluffy slippers, Enna tiptoed downstairs. As she got to the turn in the stairs there was a crash, the sound of breaking glass. Enna froze, and a moment later Wes came down the stairs. Then Mum was there; she slipped an arm round Enna, watching Wes as he undid the bolts and deadlocks and opened the door.

He looked out, carefully. Looked one way, then the other. 'Nothing . . . ' he said, then: 'No, look at that.'

The café was a basement café; that was the special thing about it. Now they looked down to the entrance and they saw a mess of earth and flowers—those nice, bright, multi-coloured primrose things Mum had put in a window box inside the railings at the top of the steps. She did her bit to make the street look cheerful, Mum did. The box had tipped over, spilling everything out, and smashed the café window.

'That's not an accident,' Wes said. Around them, Surrey Street was silent.

'Oh, my God,' Mum said. 'What's going on?' As Wes put his long, lean arms around her, Mum opened her arms for Enna, and Henry appeared at the door just in time to be included too. Even Connie, who was on record as saying being cuddled by your mum was totally *gross*, sort of sidled up to the rest of them, and the whole family stood there, swaying slightly, in each other's arms.

Chapter 7

A Matter of Perspective

There was music in the box room. It was more of a box than a room, Enna thought, but it was where Wes went when he and his guitar needed to be alone together. He'd boarded up the broken window and now Mum was downstairs, clearing up. Henry was out at his computer club, and the house had an empty feeling. Enna even thought of giving a tap on Connie's door, but she imagined her like she'd seen her sometimes, in her best jeans and her latest top, gazing at the mirror. She would be turning her face that way and this as if she couldn't get it right, and if Enna chanced to interrupt her . . . ? Maybe not.

Enna stood at the box room door and listened. She didn't know if Wes was good on the guitar, but it gave her a curious feeling—sort of wistful and cosy at the same time. Enna knocked, quite quietly.

'Yeah?' As she tiptoed in, Wes laid his guitar down.

'Don't stop,' Enna said. 'It's nice.'

'Oh, I'm not really playing— just thinking,' Wes said. 'You're a bit of a thinker, aren't you?'

'Mmmm. Sometimes.'

'Like now?' Wes pushed the

guitar case off a tea chest, making a place she could sit.

'Don't know . . . Everything's strange, all of a sudden. It was bad enough, just thinking about moving. But now . . . Is that what *you're* thinking about?'

'What I'm thinking . . . is . . . Too many things have happened all together. The bank, calling their loan in. The estate agent. And these letters.'

'Letters? More than one?' said Enna.

'Two weeks ago, the first one . . . We didn't think much about it at the time. It sounded quite friendly, that one. Just: if you would consider selling your house and café, we'd be glad to hear from you.' He dragged a fingernail over the guitar strings, so they jangled. 'I wish we hadn't thrown it away. We could trace where it came from. There was a box number, see?'

'Do *you* like Surrey Street?' said Enna.

Wes frowned. 'Yeah, I do. But . . . you know how it is. Shops closing. People moving out. The whole place feels sort of . . . ' He made a hopeless gesture.

'Sad,' said Enna.

'Sad . . . ' Wes nodded. 'Chrissie's done her best to keep it cheered up, with the café—a lick of bright paint round the door, and the sign, and that window box above the steps. And that's what they had to come and spoil: the window box. Whoever it is, they must hate our flowers.'

'Why?' said Enna, thinking of the shattered window. 'Who hates flowers so much?' Enna stared at the wall. She wasn't sad now; she was angry. As she stared, her eyes went out of focus, and suddenly the peeling plaster seemed to jerk into a shape she knew. It was only an instant, and when she blinked it was gone. It could have been just a memory of the first time, when she'd felt this angry, the first time she'd seen the Dood.

This time, in her mind, he wasn't grinning, or winking. He was looking straight at her, as if to say, *Well, what are you going to do?*

'You OK?' said Wes.

'Yes,' said Enna. 'Just remembered. There's somebody I arranged to meet, that's all.'

'Where are you?' Enna was speaking out loud, though she was in an empty room. Henry's bedroom, in fact. She'd looked under the mattress, where he'd hidden the paper last time—but her baby brother was too smart for that. She was just wondering where he might have hidden the picture of the Dood when she heard a beep in the street—Henry! One of the mums from the computer club had run him home. Enna shoved the mess back into piles and she was sitting on the landing by the time he stumped upstairs.

'Hi,' she said brightly. 'How was computers?'

Henry narrowed his eyes. 'Have you been in my room?'

'We've got to speak to the Dood!'

'Oh yes—like last time?'

'It'll be different, I know. I had this feeling . . . What have you done with the drawing?'

'You *have* been in my room,' said Henry. He patted his pocket. 'Waste of time. I've got it here.'

A minute later they were back in Enna's bedroom,

staring at the paper on the floor. Like last time, it was just a doodle.

'Well?' said Henry.

'Ssssh!' she hissed and just then the lines seemed to twitch. It was hard to say what changed. It was still just loops and tangles but all of a sudden they were taut and quivering, like elastic. Then the whole picture shifted, like a person turning over in their sleep.

'You're there!' gasped Enna.

'Hold on . . . ' The Dood seemed to pull himself tight, and shut his eyes; he gave a wiggle and suddenly there he was, standing upright.

'Wow . . . ' Henry took a step back; his eyes went wide and Enna felt his hand slip into hers. Then he steadied himself. This was better than football stickers, his look said . . . though maybe not quite as good as Shapeshifter 3.

The Dood turned and treated him to a low bow, fanning up his wings a little as he did. 'That feels better . . . Now, what's going on around here?'

'Wait a moment!' Henry put in. 'How do you know he's a good guy? He could be a demon or something.'

'Little boy . . . ' The Dood dropped his voice a pitch and made it boom slightly. 'LITTLE BOY . . . !' He gave that wet-dog shudder and in front of their eyes stretched up and out and sideways until he was as big as Henry. 'How DARE you!' the Dood said, looking him straight in the eye.

But Henry didn't move a muscle. Enna gaped. Love him or no, he could be one cool customer, her kid brother. 'Aren't you afraid of me?' the Dood said in an echoey voice. 'I can get bigger!'

Henry looked him up and down. 'But you get fainter,' he said.

'Ah . . . ' said the Dood. He looked down at himself. 'You noticed.' He shrank down to half size, and his lines went clear and sharp again. He looked embarrassed.

'Let's be friends,' said Enna. 'I mean . . . you *aren't* a demon, are you?'

'Demon? Huh!' The Dood's face, always wrinkled, seemed to crumple into worried lines. Suddenly he sprang upright. 'Demon! I'll give you *demon* . . . ' Fast as a cat, he ducked behind Henry. *Crash*. As they looked, the Harry Potter alarm clock somersaulted off the bedside table. As it hit the ground, it went off. Enna grabbed it, and saw the Dood leap for the mirror on the wall, which started swinging dangerously.

'Stop it!' said Enna. 'Mum'll hear!'

The Dood sat on one end of the mirror, dangling his feet. 'If I was a demon,' he said, 'then I'd smash things. You've heard of poltergeists, haven't you?' He swung his feet faster, like a kid on a swing. 'Take it back,' he said.

'OK, OK. I take it back.'

The Dood dropped down and landed soundlessly. 'I'm not a demon. I'm . . . ' His face creased up again. 'What *am* I?'

'Are you a Shapeshifter?'

'Henry! Sssh . . . '

'What *am* I?' the Dood said again. 'That's the

44

question. One I've spent a lot of time thinking about . . . *out there*.'

'Out there?'

'In the Margin. It's a terrible thing,' the Dood said, 'having an enquiring mind. I mean: what *am* I . . . if it takes someone like you to make me real?' He clasped his head with his hand. 'What would I have been, if Aelfric hadn't drawn me in the first place?'

'You mean . . . I didn't make you up? This Al Frick . . . ?'

'Aelfric. Young monk, long before your time . . . ' He trailed off, gazing into the distance.

'Did he . . . Did he doodle you too?'

'A different class of doodling. A fine illuminator, Brother Aelfric was. Or would have been. Ah well . . . ' he sighed. 'We don't get to choose our ways through. Someone draws one of us—sometimes just by accident, like you. You see the problem?'

Enna shook her head.

'What am I? That's the problem. *Marginalia*, that's what Aelfric's abbot said: Latin for things drawn in the margins, when the monks were copying out the Bible. I don't suppose you speak Latin . . . ? No? Pity, we could have had an intelligent conversation.'

'Marginalian!' Henry piped up. 'You're an alien!'

'*Alien?*' The Dood frowned.

'An alien is a thing from Outer Space,' said Enna.

'Ah . . . The space . . . outside. Yes, not bad, not bad. That's one way to describe The Margin.'

There was something about the way he'd said *The Margin*. You could hear the capital letters. Henry was leaning forward, eyes bright. 'Where is it? What's it like?'

'Don't ask!' the Dood snapped. Then he turned to Enna. 'But you're upset, I can feel it. Some trouble hanging over your family, am I right?'

Enna nodded. She picked her words carefully. If he didn't know *alien*, would he know *estate agent*? The Dood rested his beard on his hand and pondered.

'And so . . . Wes thinks somebody is trying to make us leave the street, and we don't know who they are, because he lost the letter, and . . . And we don't know what to do.' In the hush that followed, the Dood was so still that he seemed like a drawing again.

'I can help you,' he said.

'Help us? How?'

'I'm not sure . . . yet. But you have to find out who they are, these people. And I think . . . No, wait!' He looked up and a sly look crossed his face. 'If I help you, will you help me?'

'How?' said Henry.

'My keyhole, the way through—the picture, I mean. Give it to me.'

From the corner of her eye, Enna saw Henry's hand creep to the paper, ready to grab it if the creature made a move. 'Please,' the Dood said. 'You don't know what it means to me. If anything happened to it . . . '

'You couldn't get back?' said Henry.

'Exactly. Or if I was . . . out there—I could never get back here.'

'I could draw you again,' said Enna.

'Never. It was an accident first time. And you

46

aren't—excuse me if I say—an *artist*.' Suddenly the Dood was leaning forward—no, he was down on one knee, in front of Enna. He reached out a hand; as it touched her, she startled. It was light, like the brush of a feather, light but also strong. 'Imagine it,' he said, in a hushed voice. 'Imagine all that time out there, in the Margin, waiting for somebody, anybody, to imagine you. And every year that passes—every century—you feel yourself moving slower. Getting fainter . . . ' His voice was very small now. He looked up at her. 'This world of yours is the only life we get.'

'You mean you want to stay here?' said Enna.

'No, no, I couldn't. Not all the time. Not real enough.' His features crumpled into a worried tangle. 'I need you,' he said. 'So . . . I help you—you help me. Is that a bargain?'

Enna looked at Henry. Henry looked at Enna. 'Yes,' they said.

'Thank you. And . . . you could call me Inkle, if we're friends.'

'Inkle? You mean, like *Uncle*?' said Henry.

But the Dood was serious. 'Aelfric . . . Aelfric called me lots of things. Inkwiggle. Inklethin. Little Inkling. But mostly, just Inkle. Will you?'

'Inkle,' they said together.

'Then . . . ' The Dood sprang up and fanned his wings above him. 'Then I will help you. This *letter* you speak of . . . You have messengers, who carry such things?'

'Postmen?'

'Post Men! Good. I have a plan . . . '

Chapter 8

The Black Hole

Enna had not really seen the Dood moving. When she'd tried to catch him, there'd just been a flick and he'd been gone. Now she saw how it was done. As they made for the door together—him and her and Henry—the Dood sort of flowed towards the crack, like water that could trickle through.

'I'll go first,' Enna said. 'Make sure there's no one in sight.'

Out on the landing, the Dood crouched low, wings folded flat against him. 'Wow,' Henry said. 'How do you do that?' The Dood had shrunk flat against the wall, then down, into the dust zone where the Hoover couldn't reach. For a moment he could have been a piece of tangled string, then . . . gone, quick as a piece of twanged elastic. 'Over here,' his voice came, from the stairs. Enna led the way down to the Black Hole.

Mum believed in recycling. That was the theory, anyway. Newspapers, all the paper waste from the café,

cornflake packets, envelopes—it all went in the cupboard underneath the stairs, so they could take them to the recycling place in the Tesco car park. Except that there was such a heap in there, no way could anybody take it all, and it seemed a waste of effort to take just a few. So things went in the cupboard, and nothing came out—like a Black Hole, Wes said, but he said it kindly. One day, he promised, he would really get stuck in and clear it out. Honest.

Enna prayed he hadn't just done it today.

He hadn't. Even the Dood gave a gasp at the sight of the mass of paper. Next moment, he was in there. With one leap he landed on an old brown envelope and crouched flat, a formless scribble. Then he was burrowing downwards through the heap.

'He'll never find it,' Enna groaned. 'Look at the stuff!' She tried to believe that somewhere down there was a letter with that PO Box number on it—assuming that Wes had chucked it in the recycling bin, and that he hadn't torn it into shreds, and that . . . No, there were too many things that could have gone wrong to bear thinking about. And even if the Dood did find it, what did he intend to do?

Five minutes later, Henry looked at her. 'Do you think he's OK in there?' The paper hadn't stirred.

'Dood?' Enna called, softly. 'What did he call himself? Inkie?'

'Inkle.'

'Inkle?' they both called. No reply. It was like watching someone dive into a pool and vanish without trace.

'He could take *years*,' said Henry. Then there was a footstep on the stairs.

'What's going on?' said Connie. 'What are you two up to?' She stared into the cupboard. *Don't come out, Inkle*, Enna prayed. *Not now, please.* Connie looked from Enna to Henry, and back to Enna again. 'You're nuts,' said Connie. 'Mum's getting worried about you, you know that? Anyway, she wants you in the café. Now.'

It felt like evening in the café, what with the broken window boarded up and the lights on. There didn't seem to be any customers, either, and the woman talking to Mum was a police officer. 'It's hard to prove,' she was saying. 'It *could* have been deliberate. This kind of thing is usually kids.' She looked up and caught sight of Enna and Henry. 'Have either of you noticed anything . . . out of the ordinary lately?'

Enna looked at her face—being patient was part of her job, but she looked busy. It had been hard enough trying to tell Mum about the Dood, but this lady . . . ? No way. Enna shook her head.

'Threatening phone calls in the middle of the night?' Wes said. 'I'd say that's out of the ordinary.'

'Could be coincidence. You said yourself they didn't *exactly* make a threat. Got any aggrieved customers, have you?' They looked around. Right now, they didn't have any customers at all.

'What are they going to do?' said Henry when the policewoman left. 'Are they going to do a stake-out?

50

They could use the empty house across the road, and put men with guns . . . '

'I don't think so,' Mum said. 'They said call them if it happens again.' And she laid her head on Wes's shoulder, as if she was really tired, and let him give her a tight squeeze.

'Is it OK if we go upstairs?' said Enna. 'Me and Henry are playing a game.'

'That's nice.' Mum raised her eyebrows. 'Run along.'

Back in the Black Hole, when they got there, nothing stirred. Enna leaned in and whispered, but there was no reply. She started turning over magazines, but it was no good: there were thousands in there, and in every single one he could be between any of fifty pages. It was no good at all. There was nothing they could do but wait.

'You've got the paper, haven't you?' she said to Henry. He patted his shirt pocket. 'Good. Keep that pocket buttoned. He's bound to come back to the picture. Don't take it out, not even to look. And stay in sight of me.'

Mum must have been pleased, to see the two of them together all that evening. Come Henry's bedtime, Enna even offered to read him a story. 'Thanks,' said Mum, 'that's really thoughtful of you.'

But there was no sign of the Dood. By the end of the bedtime story he still hadn't shown. 'I'll look after the paper,' said Enna as she tucked Henry in.

'Why you? It's mine.'

'It was mine first.'

'Finders keepers,' Henry said. 'Anyway, *he* put it in my room.'

'I drew him,' said Enna. 'Give it back,' and she grabbed for the shirt. Henry held on to one sleeve, tight. 'Anyway, *you'll* fall asleep.'

'So will you.'

'I won't. I'll watch all night.' She gave the shirt a tug.

'Let go. You'll tear it.'

'*You* let go!'

'No!'

'What's going on here?' There was Mum in the doorway. 'I knew it was too good to last. What's the argument?'

Enna looked at Henry; Henry looked at Enna; they both looked at Mum. 'Nothing,' they both said. Henry let go of the shirt.

'Thanks,' said Enna, as Mum closed the door. 'He's our secret, isn't he?' But as she went to her room, she couldn't help adding under her breath: 'But he was mine first!'

In her room, she slipped the paper inside a clear plastic zip-up folder and fastened it tight. There, even the Dood couldn't squirm through that, surely. Wherever he was—on that side or on this—he would come to the plastic and stop, and she'd see him. Enna propped it up beside her pillow, where the light from the window would catch it, and she settled down to watch all night.

There was a tap on her shoulder. Enna jumped. She'd been in her old bedroom, the one she'd slept in in their old house years ago. And she daren't look up. She knew what she would see there—the horrible clock, the one her nan had sent her just before she died. It had a fat face and pink spots on its cheeks and a smiling mouth and—the terrible thing—two eyes that flicked left-right-left-right as it ticked. Three-year-old Enna had buried her head under the pillow, and when Mum had heard her crying the clock had been taken away. Every now and then, since then, Enna still had this dream.

Dream . . . Oh no! She'd been asleep. There was light at the window—it was morning. Enna could have slapped herself.

'Wake up,' said the papery voice by her ear. She rolled over and there was the Dood. His outlines looked a little tangled, as if he'd been up all night.

'By the Holy Kneebone!' he said, and slumped on the pillow beside her. 'This world of yours . . . Why didn't you tell me it had so many words in it?'

'You didn't read it all, did you? Even grown-ups don't read most of that stuff.'

'Of course I did,' the Dood said smugly. 'I learned a great deal. Did you know there is a Special Offer on metal chariots at Marsh Street Auto Dealers?'

'Never mind that. Did you find the letter?'

'Oh yes, I found it hours ago. PO Box 357. Do people live in boxes nowadays?'

'Not the ones we're looking for,' said Enna. 'Is there the name of a town?'

'Selford . . . Is that near here?'

'Near here? It *is* here. They're somewhere local. Have you got the letter?'

'Sorry. It was all ripped up in pieces. Don't look at

me like that. Have you any idea how hard it was to . . . ?'

'OK, OK,' said Enna. She was imagining telling this to the policewoman, and her heart sank. 'What now . . . ?'

'This box . . . ' the Dood said.

'Oh, right. What are you going to do—fly there?'

For a moment the Dood ruffled up his wings, but it wasn't a grand display like that first time in Enna's bedroom. The wings hung at half mast, sadly, then he folded them again. 'Sorry,' he said. 'They're ornamental. Not big enough to fly with. He just liked drawing wings, did Aelfric.' And he sighed.

'Anyway,' said Enna, 'it's a box number. We don't know where it is.'

'Aha!' the Dood said, perkier again. 'But the Post Man does.'

'The Post Man?'

'Remember what I said: I have the plan. You post me. In a letter.'

'Post *you*?'

'Post the picture. And when it gets there I come out from it . . . and find out where they are.'

'Great,' said Enna. 'But . . . how do you get back *here*?'

The Dood put his chin in his hand, just like the first time she had seen him. 'You haven't grasped it yet, have you?' he said. 'We just need another keyhole. Then I can go out there . . . and in here. In here . . . and back out . . . Through the Margin. It'll be like having a tunnel right from here to there.' He grinned, pleased with himself, then paused. 'It's got to be an exact copy of this one, though. Exactly exact.'

Enna's heart sank. Then it came to her. 'No problem!' she said. 'I can do it . . . in ten minutes.'

'How?' the Dood said. 'Pardon me saying but . . . you can't draw.'

'Trust me,' said Enna. And to her surprise he did.

Chapter 9

Big Mack

'Tell me!' the Dood's voice whispered, from the bag on Enna's back. She stopped by the corner shop window and pretended to be looking at the postcards saying Room To Let. She could feel him moving back there, through her sweater and the bag, a funny trickling feeling. 'This *copier*,' he said. 'How does it work?'

'By light. A bit like a photograph. No . . . ' She felt him squirm with impatience. 'A bit like magic.'

'Ah!' he said. 'That's all right, then. But I think I'll watch from the other side, just in case.' It was a moment before she realized what he meant. *Out There . . . the Margin*: they were just words.

'This Other Side place . . . ?' she said.

'Remember what I told Henry: don't ask. Don't think about it.'

'Why not . . . ?' But there was no answer. 'Anyway,' she said, 'I'm worried. What if anything went wrong?' In her mind's eye she saw the photocopier gobbling up the paper, ripping it to shreds. 'You couldn't get back.'

'Exactly. If anything went wrong . . . and I was over *here* . . . ' He shivered.

'What then?' said Enna.

'Think . . . Imagine being me—go on, look at me.

Now look at you. How big you are. How real. And you're only a little one. Think of all the others! At least you *notice* me.'

'I'll look after you,' said Enna.

In her bag, the Dood went spiky. 'Huh,' he said. 'Like you'd look after a fish out of water.' There was a little tussle in the backpack as he prised the plastic folder open, then he gave a wriggle and it was still. Strange, the bag wasn't any lighter, but it had an empty feeling with him gone.

'Well, young Enna. What can we do for you?' Mr Sideriou boomed in his usual way . . . or almost. He had a tired look in his eyes, as if he'd had a bad night, and his moustache drooped more than usual. 'Photocopy?' he said. 'Ah! No problem. Don't tell me: this is for your homework? Oh . . . ' As he looked at the page a puzzled look crossed his face.

'Uh . . . it's for Art,' said Enna.

'Well, then, we will make it beautiful for you. There!' Mr Sideriou held the photocopy up to the light. 'No, no, not straight. Ah, nothing goes right today. We can do better!' And he fiddled with the machine again, sighing a little as he worked.

Just then the door chime dinged behind them. Jenny Aspidistra swept in. 'That's it!' she said, to everyone in general. 'We should start a campaign. Save the Street! We'll need posters, and—Oh, Mr Sideriou, what's the matter?'

'Nothing. Just a bad luck day.'

'Mr Sideriou,' said Jenny, 'you are not alone. You know what happened at the café . . . ? Oh,' she stopped in midstream. 'Enna! Your mum just told me about last night. I just want you to know, we're right behind you. We could have a protest march, like in the Sixties. What do you think, Mr S?'

He gave a sad shrug. 'I don't know. We don't want any trouble. Here . . . ' He handed Enna the copy, and the original, but he wasn't really looking at her now. 'Run along now. No charge,' he said vaguely, then called after her. 'Tell me what mark you get for the Art.' Outside, by the post box, Enna dug in her bag. She'd found an envelope and addressed it, ready; she'd borrowed a stamp from the drawer where Mum kept them. All she had to do was slip the photocopy in and post it. For a moment, though, she hesitated.

'Dood?' she whispered to the paper. The photocopy was a little fainter than her doodle. Could it really do the magic thing? Enna wasn't sure. 'Inkle?' she said. 'Am I doing the right thing? Are you there?' But there was no answer. She put her hand on her bag, where the original was, wishing she could feel that little quiver. It just felt like paper. She would have to trust herself. She licked the envelope, gave it a pat for luck, and dropped it in the box.

'Hi,' said a voice behind her. Nico! 'What's that? A love letter?' Enna paused. She had a choice: try to explain, or punch him. She tried the punch; he ducked and they chased each other through the alley, into the back yard.

'That's better,' said Nico. 'Everybody's been foul today.'

'Maybe Jenny's right,' said Enna. 'Maybe something's happening . . . What did your uncle mean?'

'Weird stuff. This man calls yesterday, says he's from the water company and can he check the pipes. This morning, Uncle looks in the basement and there's a flood down there. Everything ruined. Then he twigs: the water company don't work at weekends, do they?'

'Have your folk had strange phone calls?' Enna said.

'How did you know?' Nico frowned. 'Oh, leave it. That's all grown-ups' stuff. Let them sort it out. Let's explore.' He grinned, and the cloud over Surrey Street lifted. Maybe he was right, thought Enna—it was grown-ups' business. 'The caveman place again?' she said.

'Let's go the other way—it's harder. Come on, last one up the wall's a wally.' One minute's scrambling later, perched on the ledge, Nico had to admit that Enna wasn't much of a wally after all.

The first couple of gardens were easy, as long as you ignored the grit that hurt your hands and knees, and the spiders . . . 'Now,' Nico whispered, 'this is the good bit.' In front of them, the rock bulged out, and there was a sloping roof built right up to it, blocking off the ledge. It didn't have walls, exactly, but the plants grew up the trellis round it, so thick that it was like an outdoor room. 'Either we go up high,' said Nico, 'and use the ivy, or jump down in the yard and run. Move fast and the witch won't see you.'

'Witch?' said Enna.

'You know, the one who lives with the woman who was in the shop. I've seen her sitting in there, burning incense.'

'That's Maggie Aspidistra. She does meditation. She's OK.'

'She's peculiar. You've got weird friends.'

'Yeah,' Enna said. 'Like you!' and they both laughed. And stopped. Somewhere near, there were voices shouting. 'What's that?'

'Don't know. Sounds like they're having a fight in the squat.' Nico's eyes lit up. 'Let's go and see.'

'We can't . . . ' said Enna, but Nico had already dropped off the wall. Five bounds and he was up the wall opposite. 'Come on, Little Miss Sensible!' he called. Enna jumped. She couldn't help snatching a look at the meditation room, though she felt she shouldn't. All the years she'd known the sisters, they'd never taken her to see their private place, out here. She looked . . . but it was empty. Enna ran.

In ten seconds she was up with Nico. They edged on along the rock ledge, then shrank in the cover of the ivy, looking into the back yard of the squatters' house. There was a mess of broken things, and the sideway gate hung open, and the window at the back gaped wide.

Crash. A mattress heaved out of an upstairs window. Then a television. As it shattered in the yard, there were voices raised from inside, really angry or afraid. There was a man in the window now, not like any of the squatters she had seen before.

The squatters, people said, were harmless. No one in the street had been pleased when they moved in, and everyone grumbled at the parties, but after a year or so people had to agree that they hadn't done anybody any harm. A couple of them came into the café now and then. First time, some of the older customers looked a bit uneasy, what with the shaved heads and nose studs— but then the squatters grinned at Mum and asked for a cup of tea and before long they were sitting down to a plate of Jenny Aspidistra's seriously wholemeal scones. Anyway, the older people said, it was a shame for a good house to be left with no one in it, and the owner didn't seem to care.

Until now, that is. The man in the upstairs window was no squatter. He had a black leather jacket, and a shirt and tie. He was big, she could see that, and there was something about him that was scarier than the shouts and bangs. He was looking out, sort of casual, at the wreckage in the yard. He took a puff on a thin cigarette and stubbed it on the window sill, then flicked it out into the yard.

'Look,' Enna whispered. 'The cigarette! Remember? At the empty house . . . ' They looked at each other. 'Let's get help.'

'Brilliant!' said Nico. 'Make for the sideway. If he sees you, don't stop running. Ready? Now!' Nico jumped. And landed on a broken plank, that cracked. He stumbled, then was running. But the man upstairs had heard. As Enna balanced on the wall, their eyes met, almost level, and his teeth bared in a kind of snarl. Then she had dropped, and didn't look back until she was through the sideway and out on the street.

'Enna!' There was a small crowd gathered, watching, not sure what to do. 'Enna! What are you doing?' It was Wes.

'Nothing! I mean, just looking . . . Wes, they're

breaking things in there!' Then the front door slammed open and three or four squatters came stumbling out. One of them was bleeding, with his arms shielding his head. Behind them came the man in the black jacket and another, leaner, hard-faced. They stood on the steps with arms folded.

'I know him!' Nico whispered. 'The thin one. That's the man from the water company!' But Wes was already pushing forward through the crowd.

'You!' he called. 'Have you got a court order to be doing this?'

'What's it to you?' The man in the jacket stepped forward. He had a big square sandpapery face and his voice had a Scottish edge to it. Not loud, but dangerous.

'Those kids in there have got some rights,' Wes said, and there was a little ripple from the crowd. 'If you've used violence . . . '

'No violence,' said the big guy. 'They just slipped on the stairs, OK?' He took a step onto the pavement. But Wes didn't budge.

'Who are you working for?' Wes said.

'The owners.'

'Who are they? And who are *you*?'

For a moment the big man loomed over Wes, then he stubbed a cigarette against the wall. At the door, the thin one was fixing a big steel padlock. 'If I was you, I'd keep my nose out of this,' said the big one over his shoulder. 'I'll make sure you do.' He nodded to his mate and they climbed into a car and revved away.

'As for you two . . . ' Wes looked at Enna and Nico.

'I don't know what to say. If I tell Enna's mum she'll go crazy.' He looked at Nico. 'Your family won't be too pleased, either. You just run on home and I won't mention it . . . this time.'

'You were brave,' said Enna, when Nico was gone.

'I was lucky,' said Wes with a lopsided grin. 'That guy was ugly. Big Mack!'

'Big Mack? Is that his name?'

Wes grinned. 'No, but it kind of fits, doesn't it? Beefy, greasy, and not good for you.' Wes was a fierce vegetarian. He rumpled Enna's hair. 'What are we going to do about you? You'll get yourself in trouble. Was it that Nico?'

'No! It was both of us. And we were just exploring.'

Wes looked at her, not angry now, as if he'd just seen her for the first time. 'You could have got hurt. Those are dangerous people.'

'Are they the ones who broke our window?'

'Don't know. You might have something there.' He put a long arm around her and steered her home. 'I won't tell Mum,' he said, 'if you promise never again.' Enna drooped her head in something like a nod. 'If we could just find out who's behind it,' Wes said, half to himself. 'Even just a name.'

Enna bit her lip. It would be so good to tell Wes about the Dood. She wanted to so much that it almost hurt. But no, she couldn't, till they had some information. When the Dood came back. Not yet.

Chapter 10

The Glory Box

Then nothing happened. It was Monday. It was time for school, and it was just like any other Monday breakfast time. Enna couldn't understand it. After all the drama of the weekend, how could they just . . . go on? The Dood was in the post, she knew that. When would he get there? Lunchtime? She could hardly eat her packed lunch for thinking of it. She kept the picture with her in her bag, and glanced at it any time she could be sure that no one else was looking. The last thing she needed was twenty people in the playground saying, *Ooh, what's that?* Apart from anything else, she had a feeling that the Dood might rather enjoy it, and start showing off.

By the end of the day, there'd been no sign of movement in her bag. When Katie and Jen in her class asked her back after school, Enna made up an excuse about having to help Mum in the café. All she wanted to do was go home and wait for the Dood. She couldn't stand the thought of him popping out in someone else's sitting room.

Then it was night. She watched the picture as long as she could, then fell asleep. Maybe his voice in her ear would wake her up, like last time? But it didn't. And the next day nothing happened, just the same. Maybe the Dood didn't like his keyhole being jiggled about in her bag? Should she leave it at home, in a safe place? But what would she do all those moments she just slipped her hand in her bag, to make sure the picture was there? What would she do when the thought came to her: maybe you're imagining all this, and the Dood was never there?

Passing the shop she caught a glimpse of Nico. She wanted to run in and tell him everything, all about the Dood . . . but what would he say? *I'd say you had a weird imagination.* She remembered how he'd said it. He'd think she was odd, like Jenny Aspidistra. He'd say *Let's explore! Forget it!* But she couldn't forget, not now.

Three days. Enna was staring out into the playground when a bad thought crept into her mind. What if the Dood had just *gone*? What had he ever done to make her trust him? Whatever he was, he was a tricksy sort of creature. He came out of nowhere, or out of somewhere that didn't seem to be a place at all. He'd started telling the story about Aelfric, but he never said what happened in the end. He could be making the whole thing up— how would she know?

At the end of the afternoon, Enna sidled over to Mrs Bolt. 'Please, Miss. If there was a monk called Aelfric,' she said, 'when would that be?'

Mrs Bolt gave her a puzzled look.

'I . . . I was reading a story about him,' Enna bluffed. 'I can't remember what it was called.'

'You'd better look in the library,' Mrs Bolt said. 'Aelfric? That sounds Anglo-Saxon to me. Do you remember anything about it?'

'He drew pictures. Sort of monsters, weird things. And he had to copy out the Bible, I think.'

Mrs Bolt nodded. 'Ah . . . illuminations. That's what

they called the pictures round the edges of the Bible.'
She was interested now. 'Let's have a look in the
encyclopaedia.' Five minutes later, Enna gasped. She
was looking at a picture of a page of curly jagged
writing—she couldn't make out a word, but at the start
of the page the first letter was huge and multi-coloured,
with patterns all twined around it and the picture of a
half-snake, half-man thing. It wasn't the Dood, but she
could imagine they might have been cousins, in the
weird place he came from. Pages like that, the book said,
were copied out by monks, by hand, more than a
thousand years ago, on an island called Lindisfarne.
Then one day, it said, the Vikings landed . . .

Enna looked up. What it all meant, she didn't know.
But the Dood wasn't making it up.

She got home that afternoon with all the books she
could find on monks, and Anglo Saxon times, and most
of all on Lindisfarne. She cleared a space at the back of
her wardrobe, hidden by the clothes, and propped the
books up, open, round the picture, so when the Dood
came back, he'd feel at home.

When the Dood came back? Or *if*? She took a clean
page from her notebook and, in her best purple felt pen,
printed: COME BACK, INKLE. I MISS YOU. Then
she shut the wardrobe door as tight as it would go.

But she couldn't stop thinking about him. If all this
was true, he was centuries old, and he must have seen so
many things happening, important things. Why should
someone of over eleven hundred care about someone of
eleven, in a place like Surrey Street? The more she
thought, the more she had a heavy feeling in her mind.

* * *

'Oh my, why the sad face?' There was Jenny Aspidistra, in the doorway of her shop. 'Bad day at school?'

Enna shook her head, but Jenny crouched down to look her in the eye. 'We haven't seen you here for ages. I think we could find you a glass of homemade lemonade.'

'Thanks,' said Enna. 'You haven't got any Coke, have you?'

Jenny laughed. She remembered Enna's face wincing from her lemonade last time. 'Just for you. Come on into the Glory Box.'

Somewhere back among the ranks of clothes—three or four things to a hanger, and every hanging rail packed tight—was Maggie Aspidistra. She was the indoor one of the pair, and moved among the piles like a wily animal that liked it best at night. She seemed to know every inch of the chaos, so if a customer asked, 'Have you by any chance got a violet tie-dye kaftan?' she would be off in a beeline, burrowing, and back in a minute with the very thing in her hand. If Jenny was big and bright, with wide flowery skirts and long hair that would still turn orange every few weeks, Maggie was quiet and sharp, in dark crushed velvet, and she'd let her short-cropped hair go grey. When Enna was small she'd been a bit afraid of Maggie—Nico was right: there *was* something witchy about her—but then there'd been the feather boa and they'd been friends ever since.

There were no chairs in the Glory Box. You just prodded the heaps into a kind of nest, and sat. Enna had never been into the rest of the house—certainly not the special place in the yard. Thinking of herself and Nico sneaking by made her feel sort of funny, now.

Jenny came in with the Coca Cola. As she brushed past, a rack of hangers jangled and a big brown coat with shiny buttons slithered down to lie beside Enna, like a dog. 'Don't mind that,' Jenny said. 'Vintage 1968 ex-army greatcoat. For a rather little soldier. Can't get rid of it. It might suit Henry one day . . . ' Enna didn't smile.

'My, you do need cheering up,' said Maggie. 'You need something bright to wear. You used to love dressing up.'

'Thanks,' said Enna stiffly, 'but I *am* eleven.'

'Sorry, sorry,' Maggie smiled. 'Well, *we* do dressing up, don't we? Some evenings when we're feeling old. You should see us. Your sister, she was a fiend for the princess costumes.'

'She still dresses up,' said Enna. 'Only it isn't a game.'

Maggie peered at her. 'Is that what's the matter? Family?'

There was something in her voice that made Enna look her in the eye. Grey eyes, but sort of sad and kind. They made Enna think that maybe she'd had a difficult family too. 'It's Inkle,' she said. 'I think he's gone . . . '

'Inkle? He's a friend?'

'No . . . or yes, but he isn't a person, not exactly . . . ' Enna stopped, embarrassed. Maggie Aspidistra was still watching with the same slight sideways smile. 'This is going to sound mad,' said Enna.

'Oh, we can do *mad*,' said Jenny. 'We're used to it.' And Maggie smiled so simply that Enna knew: if anyone could understand, she would.

It must have taken twenty minutes to tell the story, but Enna did it in one breath, or so it felt. Then she looked up, and both the Aspidistras were watching with the same thoughtful look on their faces, and they didn't laugh at her. At first, they didn't speak.

It was Maggie who nodded first. 'Yes,' she said, almost to herself, 'that figures.'

'You mean you've seen dood-things too?'

'Not exactly. But it feels right. I mean, everyone's seen faces, haven't they? In the wallpaper . . . In the carpet . . . '

'In the spaces between leaves.' That was Jenny. 'I see the Green Man sometimes, in the meditation room. Just for a moment, when my eyes go out of focus. Then I blink and it's just leaves again.'

'It's like . . . ' Maggie's forehead wrinkled. 'It's like there's something nearly coming through, only you aren't quite ready. I had a friend who could do it with tea leaves. Maybe you can do it too.'

'You mean . . . it's not crazy?' Enna said. 'Not *too* crazy?' She thought of Nico. What would he say if he could see her, with the weird sisters, being weird? People said they were slightly nuts, the Aspidistra sisters. Right now they seemed the most sensible people Enna knew.

'Just crazy enough,' said Maggie. 'And now . . . Find the girl something wild to wear!'

'No dressing up . . . ' said Jenny.

'Nothing girly,' Maggie said. She reached into the

piles and pulled out a handful of something crimson-dark and glossy. With an expert twirl she spun it to land on Enna's head. Jenny steered her to the stand-up mirror and adjusted her.

The hat wasn't girly, that was for sure. *Wild* was the word for it. One moment it made Enna think of pirates; the next, of some long-ago film star in the black and white films Mum and Wes watched on TV. None of Connie's friends would be seen dead in it. It was great.

'And don't worry about . . . you know who,' said Maggie. 'Hold on to the picture and be patient. Who knows, maybe time is different, where he comes from. He's a thousand years old, don't forget.' Enna clutched her bag. She hadn't thought of that. What if a day in our world was just a second *over there*? The Dood might be gone for *years*.

'Oh, and tell your mum . . . ' said Jenny as she reached the door, 'that we're sorry about Mrs G.'

'Mrs Grobowski? Why? What's happened?'

'Gone into a home,' said Maggie. 'It happened yesterday. They just came and fetched her.' So, thought Enna, that's another empty house in Surrey Street.

Chapter 11

The End

'Enna?' Mum's voice had that certain edge to it, like a warning light. Enna stiffened. What could she have done wrong? She'd only been home for ten minutes, just long enough to kick her shoes off and run down to the kitchen for a drink.

'This has gone too far,' Mum said. She was standing in the doorway, clutching something tightly in her hand. A piece of paper . . . No, two. She was squeezing them so hard they crumpled. 'I want an end to this nonsense. You know what I mean.' Enna tried to say something but her mouth was dry.

Mum spread the picture of the Dood out on the table.

'Mum . . . '

'No, you listen to me. I know Wes and I have been a bit preoccupied—and can you wonder at that? But at least there's somebody who's been thinking about you. I had no idea *this* was still going on.' Enna felt a coldness in her stomach. 'Don't look like that,' Mum said. 'You should be grateful to your sister.'

'Mum! Connie's been in my wardrobe? She's been spying on me?'

'She's been taking an interest,' Mum said. 'I think that's really grown-up of her. We need to look after each other at a time like this. Especially Henry . . . ' Mum paused. 'Yes, Connie's heard you and him whispering. I wouldn't mind, but you're dragging him into it, aren't you? All those times you've run upstairs to play with him . . . '

'But he's seen it too. He . . . '

'I don't think I want to hear this,' Mum said. 'It's one thing, telling yourself stories. It's another, having creepy secrets. Enna, this is weird.'

'Mum, it's only a picture . . . '

'Oh yes? Then what about this?' Mum slapped the other piece of paper on the table. Enna's note. COME BACK, INKLE. I MISS YOU.

'Oh, Enna, Enna.' Mum sank down on a chair and reached out a hand to take hers. 'Enna, you know I sound angry when I'm worried—and I'm worried now. At Henry's age, he doesn't know the difference between what's real and . . . well, fantasy. He'll believe whatever you tell him. He looks up to you.'

Enna bit her lip. What could she say? She drooped her head and wrestled with herself until the words came out.

'Sorry, Mum.'

'That's better.' Mum put an arm around her shoulder. 'Now, let's put all this business behind us. If you find yourself thinking about it, you must come and talk to me.'

'Yes, Mum.' There was a long pause. 'Can I have the picture?'

For a moment, Mum's face went red. 'Enna, you've got to stop this. It's not doing you any good. When Connie showed me that . . . place you'd built in the wardrobe, I'll admit it, I was worried. You've got to put it out of your mind. Let it go. Believe me . . . ' Mum picked up the picture and the note together and in one movement tore them both in half. She ripped the halves in half. ' . . . this is for your own good.' She ripped the halves in half and half again, then she crumpled the shreds up and dropped them in the pedal bin, with the kitchen garbage. 'There,' Mum said. 'It's over. That's the end of it.'

Enna wailed and ran out of the room.

Some time later, Enna raised her face from her pillow. It was soggy with tears and lumpy where she'd punched it, thumping it till she was exhausted and the sobbing came. There was a sound behind her and for a second she thought it might be the Dood . . . but it was Henry standing there.

'Go away,' she said.

'It wasn't me told Mum,' said Henry, in a voice so faint that Enna had to sit up and look at him.

'I know. It's not your fault.'

'Inkle's real,' said Henry. 'He's our friend. Your friend and mine together, isn't he?'

Enna pondered. Friend? How could a thing like the Dood be a *friend*? He was a sort of monster, after all.

'He was,' said Enna. 'But he's gone. He can't get back.'

'You could have made hundreds of copies,' Henry said. 'Then he'd have had keyholes all over the place.'

'I know,' said Enna. 'I know, I know!' Her eyes felt full of tears again.

'I could try and draw him,' Henry hesitated. 'He was your friend first,' he said.

Enna looked at her brother and saw his lip was quivering too. 'Oh, Henry . . . ' she sighed. He really meant it: he would try. But he was only a little kid, and not an artist, and anyway the Dood had told them it couldn't be done. Sadly, Enna shook her head. Her mum was right: this was the end of it. Enna began to cry again.

Enna made up her mind next morning: she wasn't going to cry at school. It was OK in class, because she had things to think about, but playtime was bad. She stared out through the wire fence at the backs of other people's houses and everything in the world seemed pointless and dull. All the other families in their houses, all these people in the playground, and where was she? Left out, in the middle. It helped a bit, thinking that, though it made her sad too, because they had been Inkle's words. Still, she got through the day. At the end, she started home, eyes on the pavement, when somebody called her name. There was Nico, right behind her, in his stripy uniform.

'Where've you been?' he said. 'I . . . I thought maybe you'd been grounded. I mean, after the squat . . . '

Enna shook her head.

'I've got something for you,' Nico said. And suddenly Enna felt her skin go prickly with embarrassment. Most of the girls in the class had started going on about falling in love and going out and having boyfriends, like their older sisters. It was a horrible thought: who'd want to be like Connie, always spending her money on clothes then hating them, and having a spot or split ends or some other crisis? Not her. And not Nico, surely . . . ?

He was holding out an envelope towards her. She stared at it a moment, then took it quickly in her finger tips, as if it might be hot.

'It had your name on it, that's all,' he said quickly. 'I just found it lying in the kitchen.' Who was acting weird now, thought Enna? I mean, if he wanted to give her a letter, what a stupid way to do it. Then she glanced at the envelope, and everything made a different kind of sense.

It said ENNA all right. She could only just make it out, it was written in such a curly, spiky, old-fashioned style. Where had she seen that kind of writing? Yes . . . In the book Mrs Bolt had shown her, about the monks who copied out the Bible. How could Nico have known? Besides, the envelope was torn and tatty, as if it came out of the rubbish bin. Who gave anyone love letters in an envelope like that? There was Mr Sideriou's address crossed out, and the flap was folded in, not stuck.

'I'm sorry,' said Nico, looking at the ground. 'I looked.'

'You opened it?'

'No, it was like that. What . . . what is it?' he said. The paper Enna opened out was worse than the envelope, with smears of jam and butter on it, but suddenly she gasped. It was her drawing of the Dood.

'It can't be,' she said. 'Mum tore it up.' Then she noticed: the Dood, on this paper, was lopsided, at an angle. Yes! It all made sense. The photocopier . . . She'd been so embarrassed, and wanted Mr Sideriou to hurry

up, and he'd made such a fuss about getting it *just right*.
And the first copy he'd done? He threw it in the bin
because, like this, it hadn't been quite straight. She
wanted to go back to Mr Sideriou and hug him. He'd
saved the Dood, after all. But Mr Sideriou wasn't there,
so she gave Nico a quick hug instead. Just at that
moment a couple of girls from her class looked round the
corner.

'Ooooo-eeeh! Look! Enna's got a boyfriend, Enna's
got a boyfriend . . . ' they chanted. Enna folded the piece
of paper carefully into her back pocket. Then she flew
at them, fists flailing, and they squealed and scattered
like a flock of pigeons in the street.

Chapter 12

Hell's Gate

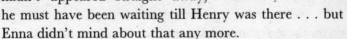

'Tar-ra! The wanderer returns!'

'Inkle!' cried Enna and Henry together. The Dood spilled out of the drawing with a kind of forward somersault, rolling himself up into a little tube of lines, then springing upright. He wrapped his wings around him like a cape and bowed low. He hadn't appeared straight away; he must have been waiting till Henry was there . . . but Enna didn't mind about that any more.

'How did you do it?' said Enna. 'The envelope . . . '

'It wasn't easy.' The Dood made a little show of modesty. 'Quill pens used to be so much easier. That was after I'd dragged the paper out of the dustbin. Which was after I'd worked out where I was, that is. All those tin cans and potato peelings. I thought: even Enna's bedroom's not as bad as this!'

'I'm being serious! I was worried. I . . . I'm sorry about your picture,' Enna said. 'I was afraid that . . . I . . . '

'You cried,' said Henry.

'Didn't!' Enna blushed, but she could have sworn that the Dood had grown a little larger—and his outlines firmer, not faint like they usually did when he grew. Was that because of her—because she'd cared? 'I thought . . .

I thought we'd lost you . . . I mean, if you came and found your keyhole gone . . . '

The Dood shrugged, but a shudder went through him. Sometimes he's like a kid, thought Enna, and the next moment he's ancient again.

'Isn't it . . . lonely out there?'

The Dood thought hard. 'I don't think you've got words for it,' he said at last.

'Why not?' Henry said.

'Because . . . Because that's how it is,' said the Dood sharply. '*You* imagine *us*; we don't imagine *you*. I mean, it's not like a whole world out there, everything going on by itself . . . not like here.'

'I don't understand,' said Enna. She looked at Henry, who was trying to pretend he did. 'You said *us*. You mean there are more like you?'

'Like me? Never! But yes, lots. And some of them you wouldn't want to think about.'

'Monsters?' Henry piped up. 'Scarier than you?'

'Oh, little boy,' sighed the Dood. All of a sudden he looked very old again. 'Mostly—if you must know—it's not frightening. It's not anything. It's cold. Especially when you don't think of us.'

'I thought of you,' said Enna.

'I could feel it. It's like . . . sunshine. We warm up, move quicker . . . '

'And if we don't think of you?'

'We . . . slow down,' he said. 'Everything gets cold . . . and vague . . . and still.' He sighed. 'I've spent a long time out there, since . . . since . . . ' He trailed off.

'You're still sad about Aelfric, aren't you?' Enna said.

'What happened?' said Henry. 'Did his mum rip your paper up?'

The Dood smiled. 'Monks don't have mums. No, no, of course they do, but they have to leave home. Aelfric lived in a great abbey with the other monks.' He gave a wistful look. 'Actually, Aelfric used to send letters home to his mum—not that she could read. She sold fish. Really proud of him, she was.' He sighed again, then looked at Enna. 'Did you really miss me?'

'You should have seen her,' said Henry. 'She hasn't been so fed up since her gerbil died.'

'You must have been,' said the Dood. 'Because you haven't asked me about the business. Aha . . . ' He settled himself down on the bookshelf with his legs crossed. 'Do I have an audience? Then I shall begin.'

The first time he looked out, said the Dood dramatically, he thought he was in Hell. No, not in Hell, but at Hell's gate, where the angels and the devils make their terrible judgement, dividing the sheep from the goats, the good from the wicked. He paused and looked at each of them, enjoying the moment.

It was a great hall, he went on, and with a greater hall beyond, where metal chariots rolled in and out with roaring sounds. As he slipped out of his paper and out through the crack in the envelope, he found himself lying on a mountain made of hundreds, no, of thousands of envelopes. Before he got to his feet, there was a jolt and with a grinding of machinery the ground beneath the pile began to move, setting the mountain sliding like a

79

rocky scree. In one direction flowed a kind of metal river, which carried the letters off in the direction of . . . what, at first he could not see. Then he made out the place where the river narrowed, shuffling them into single file, and there was a terrible machine that stamped a brand on all their faces, and creatures in the guise of men leaning over the letters throwing them with one glance into this pile or that, where other metal rivers bore them off and out of sight.

'A sorting office,' Enna said. 'It's where the postmen sort the letters.' The Dood gave her a stiff look, and decided to ignore the interruption.

'All that I saw at a glance,' he went on, 'but as I looked back—horrors!'

Now Enna saw his point, because the shifting of the pile had covered up his envelope and it was somewhere in the moving shuffling mass. So he dived in among them, fighting to read the scribblings of addresses, and each time he put up his head the belt had moved on and the end was getting nearer, nearer. Any moment now someone would see him or, if he lay low, what if his envelope went one way and he another? How would he ever find it again?

Only seconds left now, he took the risk of standing upright—like a man on a raft, he said, and mimed an action that made Enna think of surfing. And there was his envelope, just ahead of him, about to be swallowed by the great branding machine. With one leap he had leapt for it and grabbed one corner, hauling himself up out of sight beneath it, through the crack and back into the picture just as—whoomp!—the impact hit them so hard that it threw him out into the Margin like a great stone from a catapult.

'Wow,' said Henry.

'Oh, come on . . . ' said Enna. But she had to admit it: as a storyteller the Dood had style. 'What about the business?'

'I was coming to that,' the Dood said, and from there on told it straight. The next time he looked out he was careful. He left it for a long time till he was certain he'd come to a stop, then he peeped out. He was in a large room, he said, with many people bent over desks, not unlike a scriptorium.

'Pardon?' Enna said.

'Where the monks worked copying their texts—except that now . . . ' and here he dropped his voice a little, 'all the scribes seem to have books that glow like stained glass.'

'Computer screens,' said Henry, and the Dood flashed him a look: *I know, I know . . .*

The letters were piled on a desk. The Dood knew it was only a matter of time before somebody started opening them. He waited till no one was looking, scrambled out and dragged his envelope out of the in-tray, off the edge of the desk—a terrible pause as it hit the floor, and someone turned and looked . . . then turned back to her screen—then he dragged it through the crack between two filing cabinets, paused for breath, then he struggled it underneath the nearest door.

The room at the back was small, with just a thin high window, and no one came in. He spent the rest of the day making little expeditions out and back, and he started to feel safe. The people were tied to their screens or talking to machines that answered them in squeaking voices. ('Telephones,' said Henry. He was good at this game.) But it was in the private room, the Dood said, that they kept the information about Surrey Street. 'And this . . . ' he said triumphantly, 'is what I learned.'

They called themselves The Consortium. Outside in the big open office there was a lot of other business going on, and they seemed to be exchanging lots of . . . 'What is a . . . ?' the Dood said, making a £ shape in the air.

'Pounds. Money,' Enna said. 'Like gold.'

'Ah. Plenty of those. And they plan to have many more when they have done what they want to with Surrey Street.' Now Enna was listening, all ears. On the wall in the back room was a map, and on the map were all the houses, all the names of everyone in Surrey Street . . . and he could see how most of them had been crossed off, in red pen, one by one.

'The empty houses,' he said. 'The consortium has bought them all, in secret, under different names.'

'But why?' said Enna. 'They don't want to live here, do they? No one does.'

'They don't want to live in Surrey Street. They want to knock it down. They want to build . . . excuse me, but what is a *Complex*?'

'No,' Enna said. 'They can't. People would never let them. I mean, the Council . . . '

The Dood nodded. 'I recognize the name *The Council*. They have a good friend there, I seemed to hear. And in the . . . what is the place they keep the pounds?'

'The bank?'

'Yes, they have friends there too, and . . . I'm sorry, but no one seems to be the friend of Surrey Street.'

'Rubbish,' said Enna. 'There's us. And you. And now we've got to tell Wes. Straight away. Come on.' The Dood didn't move. He shook his head.

'What is it?' said Enna.

'This Wes . . . He hasn't seen me before.'

'For heaven's sake, you aren't *shy*?'

The Dood's lines stiffened. 'I don't show myself to just anyone,' he said. 'Besides, he won't believe his eyes. People don't. It'll only make trouble.'

Enna sighed. 'OK, so what do I tell him?'

'Tell him where their hideout is. Number 86 High Street.'

'High Street? But that's . . . that's in the next street.'

'Didn't I mention that?' said the Dood. Suddenly the light at the bedroom window seemed duller, as if the shadows of the offices and car parks at the back had leaned right over Surrey Street.

'OK. And you, you'd better wait here,' she said to Henry. She remembered how mad Mum had been about her *dragging Henry into this*.

'That's fine,' chirped Henry. 'I'll look after Inkle.' As she closed the door behind her, she heard Henry's voice: 'What's it like, in your Margin place? I'll show you my computer if you tell me. Go on. Please . . . ?'

Chapter 13

Trust Me

'Run me through it again,' said Wes. He looked worried, but not, Enna started to think, for the right reason. 'How do you *know* all this?' he said.

'A friend of mine . . . '

'Ah!' Something dawned in Wes's face. 'It's that Nico, isn't it? He's a nice enough kid, but you mustn't let him lead you on. He'll get you into trouble.'

It wasn't fair, and Enna felt the anger well up in her. But she took a deep breath. Now wasn't the time for an argument. She had to make Wes understand. 'It wasn't Nico,' she said. 'If you promise to listen, I'll tell you who it was.'

Wes sat back, very calm. 'I think you'd better.'

'It was Inkle. The Dood. You know I drew a picture . . . '

'Oh, Enna,' Wes sighed. 'Chrissie told me about that business. She said it was all over and forgotten.'

'But it's true! Come and see!' Whether Wes would have come with her, Enna never found out, because at that moment there was a shout from upstairs. Mum's voice. Mum sounding urgent, worried, scared. 'Wes? Is Henry with you?'

'No. Why?'

She didn't answer but they heard her footsteps, running down the stairs. When they met on the landing, she was out of breath. 'I've looked everywhere. Enna?' she said. 'Where is Henry?'

84

'He was in his room just now.'

'He was.' There was Connie, just behind Mum, looking puzzled. 'I heard the two of them talking.'

'So did I,' said Mum. 'Then I went in and . . . he wasn't there.'

'Calm down.' This was Wes in his peacemaker role. 'He'll be on the computer. Maybe he's just in the bathroom. Or . . . '

'Maybe he's hiding,' said Enna.

'No, no. I've looked everywhere. He's vanished. Enna, this isn't anything to do with you?'

Enna looked at the carpet. 'He was in his room, Mum, truly.'

'Then he must have got out in the street somehow. Connie, run out and look. Oh my God, what if somebody's taken him . . . ' Then she was shaking and her eyes were wet with tears. Wes put his arms around her.

'Easy, easy . . . ' he said.

'Things have been so weird round here lately,' Mum said. 'What's going on? Wes, let's call the police.'

As soon as she could slip up there alone, Enna closed the door of Henry's bedroom. 'Henry?' she whispered as loud as she dared. 'If this is a silly game, Henry . . . Henry?' But the room was empty; she could feel it, just the way she'd felt it when the Dood wasn't there in his picture. And that put a bad thought in her mind.

'Dood!' she hissed. 'Where are you? Come out now!'

There was a rustle at the bottom of the bed, and a very small and crumpled Dood looked out.

'What have you done with Henry?' Enna said.

'Nothing!' said a small voice. But Enna could see he was squirming. She lay down on the rug and looked him in the eye. 'This is serious. Mum's going crazy. What's happened?'

'I just told him, that's all. He wanted to know about the Margin, and the more I told him, the more excited he got, and . . . '

'And? Where is he?'

'He wanted to go there. I told him he couldn't, of course. I explained it was impossible. Or it ought to be . . . ' The Dood paused, and Enna had a dizzy feeling.

'No,' she said. 'He can't have. We—real people, I mean—can't go through. You said we couldn't . . . '

'It's never been tried,' the Dood said. 'I warned him, honestly I did. But every time I told him about one of the terrible things he'd just say, *Oh, I've seen better than that*, and show me one of his illuminated game things. He seems to like fighting monsters.'

'You're saying . . . ' Enna said it very slowly. 'You're saying . . . that Henry . . . went into the Margin? *How?*' She followed where the Dood was pointing, on the bedroom wall. Above the bed were pink chalk scribbles on the patterned paper. How many times had Mum told him not to do that when he was younger? Seeing it now, Enna felt as though the floor had dropped out at her feet.

'I tried to stop him,' the Dood said, 'but he just kept

86

drawing, and he got it right somehow. It shouldn't be possible,' he finished lamely.

Enna stared at the marks, then reached out a hand to trace them with her finger. It was Henry's outline, all right, and yet it fitted in exactly with the floral-curly patterns, as if it had always been there, waiting for this day.

'I'm sorry,' the Dood said.

There was a long pause. Enna stared at the wall. Her stupid, stupid, clever little brother! What had he done? And why, of all times, now? Downstairs, she could hear Mum's voice on the phone. Any time now that patient policewoman would be back again, and there would be explaining to do. *Explain?* she thought. *Impossible.* But a desperate thought was forming in her mind.

'We've got to get him back,' she said. 'I'm going through . . . If he can, so can I.'

'You can't,' said the Dood, but she wasn't listening. Enna was trying to push at the shape on the wallpaper, squeezing herself into the outline. She pushed and she squirmed . . . but nothing happened. Enna thumped with her fists, and nothing happened. It was just a wall.

'I told you,' the Dood said. 'Best wait for him to come back. He won't want to stay there, when he sees it. As long as the keyhole's there . . . ' He stopped in mid sentence. He was staring at the chalk marks . . . or the place where they had been. There was pink chalk on Enna's hands, and on her elbows and her knees. Not on the wall. 'Oh, dear . . . ' said the Dood.

'Oh . . . ' Enna said. There was a silence so deep that

they heard the click as, downstairs, Mum put down the phone. 'Quick, draw it again,' said Enna. But one look at the wallpaper was enough to tell her it was hopeless. The floral patterns wriggled here and there; she didn't have a clue where Henry's shape had been.

'Then you'll have to take me,' she said.

'No,' he said. 'Not safe.'

'You mean you *could*? Then do it! Henry's out there!'

'Just keep calm. I'll fetch him.'

'No, I'm coming.' The Dood glanced at his picture, but Enna grabbed it, faster than he could move.

'Careful!' he cried. 'My keyhole . . . '

'My *brother* . . . ! Take me. Or I rip up this picture too!' The Dood had swelled, bit by bit, as they were talking, and Enna was kneeling up now to keep level. 'I don't want to fight,' she said. 'Please, help me. Can I draw myself, like he did?'

'I don't think so. It could have been a fluke— incredible coincidence—his outline just fitted the pattern. You could be scribbling all day and it still wouldn't work. Or it might have been because he's so young . . . '

'What? You mean any little kid could do it?'

'Your brother isn't any little kid, is he?'

'No,' said Enna with feeling. 'He certainly isn't.'

But the look on the Dood's face had changed. A moment ago he could have been a toddler in a tantrum, stamping his little foot. In the blink of an eye, he could have been a kindly uncle. 'So you don't hate him, after all?'

'Of course I hate him. He's my brother . . . ' Enna faltered. 'But I kind of love him too.'

Outside in the street, a car pulled up. Surely it couldn't be the police already. There was a rap on the door, and Mum's voice called up: 'Enna?'

'There's just one chance,' the Dood said in a voice so small she had to bend down closer than she'd ever been. She felt his breath, if it was breath he had, like the slightest tickle in her ear. 'I don't know,' he said, 'but . . . You'll have to trust me.'

'Why?' Enna said. The Dood's eyes kept flitting to the picture. Trust him? That was his lifeline. Wouldn't he just bolt through it if he had the chance?

'Because I like you,' the Dood said. Enna could hear the voices downstairs in the hall now. 'Enna?' Mum called again.

'And . . . ' The Dood shrugged. 'What else can either of us do?'

'And if I do trust you?'

'I have to be inside the picture . . . OK, I know what you're thinking: you'd be mad to trust me, but . . . just *do*.'

Enna looked at the Dood, long and hard. She wished she was as bold as Nico. But what would Nico say about her now? He thought this was all some silly make-believe. Don't talk about it, he'd said, or people will think that you're mad. OK, so she was mad. And it would be mad to trust the Dood. So she would.

Very slowly she laid the paper down on the floor between them. The Dood didn't dive for it. 'Somewhere well out of sight,' he said. 'Where they won't find it.' She stood it up against the bookcase, edgeways on so Mum wouldn't see from the door. Quickly, she propped a lot of books and magazines around it, like her usual clutter.

'Now,' said the Dood. 'I'm going into it . . . but I won't go through.' For a moment he was a slither of lines, then he fitted the doodle perfectly. He gave his lines a little wriggle, just to reassure her he was there.

'Now,' came his voice, with an echoey feel to it, 'I'm going to try to make it bigger . . . ' And there was a shuffle and a grunting sound. The whole outline seemed to strain and swell a little, then a little more.

'I can do it,' came the Dood's voice, out of breath. 'It won't be easy, and I won't be able to speak, so listen. Listening?'

'Yes.'

'I'm going to make the outline big. As big as you.'

'What?'

'Trust me. If I can do it, I'll only be able to hold it for a second. So when I get there . . . Are you listening?'

'Yes!' There were footsteps coming upstairs.

'When I get there, you've just got to *jump*.'

90

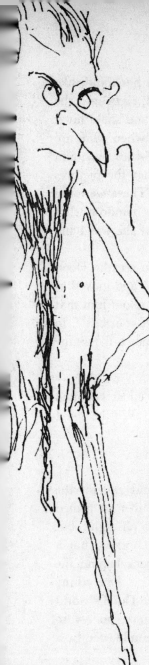

Chapter 14

A Kind of Nowhere

Enna jumped. One moment she was watching, gobsmacked, as all the Dood's outlines seemed to stretch and stretch, larger than the paper, larger than she'd ever seen him, and still stretching. All the lines that made him were straining apart and as the space in the middle got larger, the space seemed to stretch, too, like a white plastic bag goes see-through when you stretch it and it's just about to break. Through it, Enna could almost make out shapes and shadows—not the bedroom but a place beyond.

Then the outline shuddered. *I'll only be able to hold it for a second*, he had said, and the Dood's voice in her mind said *Jump!*

She was lying on the ground—hard, gritty ground, and she was cold. It seemed to be a hillside, sloping up above her, sloping down below. Both ways, it vanished into shifting mist. This was nowhere like anywhere Enna had ever been. It had to be the Margin. It was real.

What had happened? It was vague in her mind, like waking out of a dream. She had jumped, right into the middle of the space that was the Dood, and she'd hit it hard as falling into water. They say when you are drowning your whole life reels past before your eyes, and for a moment it was like that, except that the pictures in her mind weren't any life she'd lived. There were the deep reds and purples of a stained-glass window, that suddenly shattered. And the next moment she was lying there, her cheek against bare stone.

There was a groan, and she turned to see the Dood sprawled beside her. He was her size now, and looked as battered as she felt. There was something about him that seemed different, though—more solid. Of course . . . in his own world he had three dimensions, not a flat shape any more.

'Dood? Are you all right?'

He rolled over to face her. With an effort he lifted his head, then fell back, gasping. 'OK . . . Will be . . . I wish . . . '

'Yes?'

'Wish you'd call me Inkle,' he said.

'I'll try,' said Enna. She looked around and for the first time realized she was afraid. The chill mist trailed around them. This was somewhere else, all right, but that somewhere was a kind of nowhere, nothing but a stony hillside—red and gritty, like the rock behind the gardens back in Surrey Street. But bigger . . . Everything was bigger here. Enna felt as small in the Dood's world as he must in hers. There was no shelter—no ivy to cover the red rock—as if the place had been blasted by a scorching wind before it got so cold. There were shapes like trees or boulders that rose in the moving mist. Enna gasped as the air cleared round one for a moment and she saw a long profile of a face, long nose, long chin, like Easter Island statues.

'Don't be afraid.' The Dood was beside her. 'It's like this sometimes here. Try not to look.'

'Not look? We've got to find Henry.'

'And we will. Only, when you notice . . . things . . . just walk by. Try to ignore them.' Enna was staring at him, baffled. 'This is the Margin,' he said. 'Lots of the things here . . . aren't things. They're alive.'

'You mean, *like you*?' said Enna. What was the word Henry had made up: *Margin-alien*?

'Most of them are very old and slow. If you pay them attention, they—Well, take my word for it. Just don't, OK?'

All around them there was silence. Just the tiny whisper of the wind among the rocks. 'I want to go home,' Enna said. 'I want to find Henry and go home, quickly. This is a horrible place.' She got to her feet. 'Hen-ry!' she yelled, two or three times. There were tiny echoes. Then the silence.

'Curious . . . ' The Dood was speaking to himself. 'It's . . . different.'

'You do know where we are, don't you?' said Enna, faintly.

'Wait. I'm thinking. Yes . . . ' He peered around in the mist. 'It's different because of Henry. And if it's different because of him, that means he's here. And all we've got to do . . . ' He laid a hand on Enna's

93

shoulder, and it felt more real than he'd ever felt before. ' . . . is look for the signs of him. Anything you see that looks like something Henry might have thought of . . . '

'You said *don't look* . . . '

'Of course you've got to *look*. Just don't . . . think about it too much.' Great, thought Enna. How? And the image of Nico flashed in her mind. He could do it. She wished he could be beside them now.

'Well, let's start,' said Enna, and she stepped into the mist. In a couple of steps, the Dood was out of sight. 'Inkle!' she called. As she looked up, the mist thinned and there up the hillside was what might have been a boulder, in mist-silhouette. And it was watching her.

Enna screamed. The thing had eyes. And stumpy feet. It was the terrible clock face from her nightmare—only huge and grey and made of stone.

The Dood was by her side. She felt his arm across her shoulder, his other hand shielding her eyes. 'Don't . . . ' he said.

'That thing . . . ' she stuttered. 'It's . . . It's my . . . '

'Something of yours?' said the Dood. 'That figures. Just don't pay it attention,' he said, and he steered her gently away. For a second she glanced back, and the thing was there, but fading. If she kept looking, she knew, it would darken and get big again. 'Trust me,' the Dood said.

'But . . . Henry?'

'If he's near, he'll have heard you,' said the Dood, 'the noise you made then.'

'I . . . I thought you'd vanished.'

94

'I found something. Let me show you . . . ' And he led her by the hand.

The low stone walls appeared from the mist below them. They were only ruins, with no roof and two walls gone. Still, Enna could make out high thin pointed windows, like a church.

The Dood paused on the threshold, as if he might be going to knock on an invisible door . . . then he brought her in. Inside, he breathed a low sigh and let her hand fall. Very slowly, he walked towards the window.

It must have been stained glass, once, though it was hidden by grime. Enna could just make out the loops and curls of ancient writing, and the weave of colours round the sides. As she came up behind him, she could see it was a page of monkish writing—like the illumination Mrs Bolt had shown her—the Lindisfarne Gospel . . . except that down in the margin, at the start of the final paragraph, was the shape Enna knew so well . . . Brother Aelfric's *Inkwiggle* . . . *Inklethin* . . . *Little Inkling* . . . who had somehow unbelievably become her *Inkle*.

'Is this it?' she said. 'Your old keyhole?' He was nodding. 'Does it still work?'

'No, no. The page was . . . lost. But it's beautiful.'

Enna pressed her face against the glass. It was almost opaque, most of it, with just the hint of a colour—dark garnet, inky purple. Just here and there was a glint of light, and as she put her eye to one she thought she caught a glimpse not of grey mist but of distances beyond—a coastline, and white lines of breakers on the sea.

The Dood was watching her. 'Did you see it?' he said very quietly. 'The island?'

'Is that where we are? On Lindisfarne?'

'No. Can't get back there.' He looked so sad. 'Just as well we can't. All ruined. Burnt and plundered. Everyone put to the sword.'

'You mean the Vikings?' Enna said.

'Sea-wolves. Northmen, in their long ships.'

'I . . . I found out about them at school.'

'What did they tell you about them, at school?'

'How they used to sail all over, raiding and stealing. How they had horns on their helmets.'

'Actually they didn't have horns. But they looked like the devil to us.' His voice almost faded away, so Enna looked at him. But he was firm and solid, in the Margin. He was real here, but there were centuries of sadness in his eyes.

'Lindisfarne's still there, you know,' said Enna cautiously.

'No, they destroyed everything . . . '

'No, really. I've seen pictures. They rebuilt the abbey. And they've got the Gospel, all those beautiful illuminations. And . . . ' She looked at his face. 'Oh . . . I'm sorry. Aelfric . . . ' The Dood had turned away from her, gazing at the window. Enna could not go on.

'Don't worry,' the Dood sighed. 'It was over a thousand years ago. Now, let's find Henry.'

They stopped and listened, went on, stopped and listened. Now and then they called. Each time there was nothing but echoes. Then, on the fourth or fifth stop, Enna pointed.

'Look, there!'

They peered through the mist. It was a clutch of dry roots, upside down and stripped to whiteness by the wind and rain. It was only a tree. 'Sorry,' Enna said. 'I thought . . . But it wasn't.'

'Thought what?'

'I thought it was one of the things from his computer game—the octopus thing.'

'Good! There have never been trees here before. If that's what it looked like . . . Henry must have come this way.'

After that it was easier. Enna knew what she was looking for, though the slope was growing steeper, and the gravelly rock gave way and slithered off beneath their feet. In one place there was a hollowed-out basin in a dried-up stream bed that looked just like the baby bath Henry had had when he was small. Enna wished she'd taken more notice of his computer games, because there were glimpses of things in the mist that could have been creatures he'd zapped on his way to a score of hundreds of thousands. Or they might not be—there was so much clutter here—old statues tumbled sideways off their crumbling bases, faces staring upwards at the sky. By some of them the Dood paused, head lowered for a moment, then pressed on. Enna was tired now, her legs aching from the steepness of the slope, her knees bruised from the slips and scuffles. She reached out a hand to steady herself on what looked like a broken gatepost . . . and jumped back, as two slits in the wood came open and were eyes that swivelled round to gaze after her with dreadful longing. The Dood hurried her by.

'What was it?' Enna asked, some way later.

'Oh, just a small god,' the Dood said. 'Quite harmless.'

'Will he follow us?'

'It would take him years to get this far. No one's believed in him for, oh, ten thousand years, you see. That's why he's so slow.' Then they were searching again, searching and calling, for so long that Enna's feet went numb and started stumbling. She looked up at the rocks and for a moment thought she saw an opening like Nico's cave. If only she could curl up there, and be safe behind the ivy, and just sleep . . . As she started sinking, the Dood reached out an arm and took her weight. He was strong, in this world, and for a while he almost carried her. When he grew tired too, he laid her down.

Then there was silence, and they kept hold of each other's hands. And then—so faint that Enna thought she was imagining it—a sound of someone laughing. A little boy's laughter. Enna and the Dood looked at each other. 'Henry!' they both said in the same breath, and scrambled to their feet and set off at a hobbling run.

Chapter 15

Playing With Fire

The path tracked round the hillside, into crumbling gullies and up the other side, squeezing between tumbled boulders . . . but with each twist and turn the sounds got louder. Enna knew that laugh, all right. It was the way Henry chuckled to himself when he was deep in one of his computer games and getting excited, going for the best score ever—like that, only louder, funnelled up from somewhere deep among the rocks. Enna slithered down and there, under the shade of an overhang, she saw the cave mouth. Somehow the mist seemed different round here, coiling up in strands towards her. Enna sniffed; the haze around the entrance wasn't mist but smoke.

The Dood laid a hand on her arm. 'Wait!' He edged forward, peering. 'Oh, no,' he whispered. 'Not that!'

Enna came up beside him, crouching at the cave mouth, following his gaze. There, in the heart of the curling smoke, was a fierce orange glow. As it flickered and flared, the smoke rose, fell, and swirled like

 something being stirred up, arching up into shapes—wasn't that a great bird taking off with spread wings? wasn't that a bull with horns down, charging? wasn't that a savage

dancer, horribly tall and skinny, swaying? *We make a fire and dance around it*. That was Nico's voice in Enna's mind. *Then we do a human sacrifice*. No sooner had she thought it than the smoke billowed down, mixed, and mingled again.

On the edge of the smoke stood Henry, like a lion-tamer. With a sweep of his arm, he sent a tongue of smoke up and out to break against the cave wall. For a second it was a scattering herd of beasts, like something being hunted, and as he cackled with glee they seemed to brighten, breaking into sparks. He swung back to the heart of the smoke, which rose and bulked above him like a thing with massive shoulders. He laughed again, and the thing seemed to glow in reply. Yes, Enna realized with a start, it *was* a thing. It was playing, it was dancing with him, and it was alive.

'Oh no,' the Dood said again. 'He's gone and woken it up.'

'What *is* it?'

'Something very old. It was old in the Stone Age.'

'Is it . . . dangerous?'

'Don't know. No one's ever *played* with it before. Let's not wait to find out. Let's get him out of there.' He laid his hand on her shoulder. 'Now . . . We walk in, quickly but calmly. Don't pay *it* any attention.'

'What! Won't it . . . ?'

'Not if you don't encourage it. See how it loves what Henry's doing. He's making it stronger. You just walk up to Henry, take his hand, and lead him out. OK?'

'If you say so,' Enna said. They stepped into the cave.

The smoke-thing sensed them instantly. For a moment Henry was left standing as it hung above them like a mushroom cloud. A flicker of shapes passed through it— half-human, half-animal, all crouched like things stalking their prey. Then it drew in to an almost human shape. From the crown of its head stray flames became the many-branched antlers of a stag. 'Look out!' Enna shouted.

He wheeled round, confused.

'Henry! You stupid little—Everybody's been so worried . . . '

But Henry was running towards her, wrapping her in a big hug. 'I've found this brilliant thing,' he chirruped. 'You just look at it and think and it changes into—oh, all sorts of things. It's even better than Shapeshifter 3! Look at it!'

'No,' said Enna. 'Come with me.'

'But—!'

'Come on *now*!' Enna grabbed his hand, the way Mum used to when they had to cross the road.

'Let go!' said Henry, and the fire thing loomed above them, coming closer. *Don't look*, Enna told herself. *Somehow, you mustn't look*.

She yanked Henry by his hand. 'Don't run,' hissed the Dood. 'It'll feed on your fear.'

'I'm not afraid,' said Henry, then choked as the smoke poured down around them, and the cave mouth vanished in the smokescreen.

The Dood grabbed Enna's hand and towed them,

coughing, out into the cold air. 'Run!' he said, and the three of them ducked and dodged among the boulders. 'Don't look back,' said the Dood, and Enna tried not to. Just for a moment she pushed Henry out of sight, and peeked back around a corner. There was the cave mouth, and the cloud of smoke was questing round, outside it. It seemed to have smothered its fire inside the cloud, which glowed from inside, swirling as the antler-tips swished to and fro. It wasn't a cloud: it was a living thing. And just thinking about it was enough; as she looked, it turned towards her.

'I only wanted to be by the fire,' said Henry. 'I was cold. What's wrong with——?'

'Run!' the Dood said. The smoke thing was coming. There was a kind of massive sigh, a rushing in the air behind them, that was sad and terrifying at the same time. 'Here!' the Dood cried and slipped into a gully. All at once they were slithering, with a small landslip around them. With a lunge, the Dood threw himself sideways, grabbing Enna, who grabbed Henry, and he braced himself against a boulder. To one side, the rock fall clattered down, and the thing made of smoke, a wavering tower of it with an angry glow like fire at its centre, raced down after it. The three of them clung to each other, hardly breathing, until it was gone.

'That was my Shifty,' said Henry. 'It was friends with me.'

'I don't think it has *friends*,' said the Dood. 'But you were giving it lots of attention. It was getting wilder, getting stronger.'

'Is it another god-thing,' said Enna, 'like the gatepost? It's just . . . smoke.'

'Smoke?' the Dood said. 'Just smoke? Let me tell you a story. Shhh . . . ' He sat, cross-legged. 'Long, long ago—the Stone Age—there was a tribe who had a special sacred tree on a hill top. It was close to the clouds, they reasoned, so when there was a drought that's where they went to pray for rain. The whole tribe sat around it, as the old priest climbed into its branches. And almost at once the sky went dark. There was a rumbling—'

'Thunder,' Henry put in.

'Right. And the priest raised his arms, like this . . . and then—flash! Everyone was blinded for a moment—and when they looked back, the tree was blazing, and at the same moment it began to pour with rain. It was like a miracle. All they could do was stare—they were so scared and so pleased and so astonished. This great column of smoke was rising, twisting round in the wind, and it looked like—anything they could imagine.'

'Uh . . . What about the priest?' said Henry.

'Burnt to a crisp. All that was left was burning branches, which just happened to look . . . '

' . . . like antlers,' Enna said.

'You saw that?' the Dood said. 'You saw its antlers? I told you not to look.'

'I looked,' said Henry. But the Dood went on.

'These stupid humans, then, they talked and talked about it, till their wise men thought they understood. Aha, they said, the next time we want rain after that, we

103

build a bonfire and—They thought that the smoke god wanted sacrifices, see?'

'That's crazy. It was only lightning.'

The Dood sighed. 'You do some crazy things, you human beings.' The silence settled round them slowly. Somewhere far down the mountainside, the slipping stones had stopped. 'Come on,' he said. 'The thing'll be back.'

'You mean it's after us.'

'I rather think it wants Henry. Nobody's looked at it like that since the Stone Age.'

'So it *is* my friend!' said Henry.

'Personally,' said the Dood, 'I'd rather not have friends who believe in human sacrifice. Come on, let's get back to the keyhole.' And they angled back up the hillside, picking their way carefully for fear of starting stone slips, stopping every now and then to get their breath.

'How much further?' Enna panted after a while. The mist was settling silvery and chilly on their skin. Henry was whimpering slightly, pale with tiredness. He'd stopped chattering some time ago. Much more of this and he'd start sucking his thumb.

'It's somewhere round here,' said the Dood.

Enna had a sudden bad feeling. 'You mean you don't know?' she said.

'I didn't say that,' the Dood said.

'Well, *do* you?'

'Not *exactly* . . . ' he said. Henry started sobbing quietly. 'I told you: things have changed since Henry came here,' said the Dood. 'It's your fault, you humans.

You're the ones who imagine us.' But Enna had stopped listening.

'There!' she shouted. There was the half-ruined wall of the chapel. 'It was up, beyond there . . . ' Enna glimpsed the Easter Island face, but didn't look this time. She ran on, towing Henry. 'Inkle!' she called suddenly. 'Look!' There was the Dood's shape, traced on the rock in orange lichen. 'Your keyhole! Can you get us both through?'

The Dood was squinting. 'Something's not right,' he said. 'It's different.'

'You just said that things change. Quick. It could be coming . . . ' At these words, Henry started on a loud wail. 'Please!' said Enna. 'It's bound to hear him.'

'OK,' said the Dood, in a weak voice. 'But you'll have to jump together. You can't imagine what it feels like.'

'Thank you,' said Enna. 'You're very brave.' She wrapped her arms around him, and he frilled his wings around them both.

'Now,' he said, and stepped into the keyhole shape, and stretched, and stretched.

'What—?' said Henry. It was too much to explain. As Henry shrank against her shoulder, Enna squeezed him tight. The Dood was stretching, stretching to his limit, struggling to hold it . . . Enna tipped herself and Henry both in, headlong.

Falling, falling. That same tearing feeling. There was no up and no down, and strange life-pictures whirled around her. There was a door, stove in, and men in helmets, blocking a doorway. Vikings. Then they hit the ground together with a thump.

Enna opened her eyes. Yes, they'd made it, all of them: her and the Dood and Henry. They were back in the real world. The only thing was, the floor they'd crashed down onto *wasn't* Henry's bedroom floor.

Chapter 16

Mousetrapped

Enna looked up. 'Where are we? Inkle?' She still had Henry tightly in her arms.

'Let go,' he said, 'you're squeezing me.'

The Dood was stretched out on the carpet, moaning. Enna shook him. 'Wake up. What's happened?' The Dood opened his eyes, looked and shut them again.

'Hurts . . . ' he said. 'You've no idea . . . The two of you . . . '

'I know, I know,' Enna said. 'And thanks. But what's gone wrong?'

The Dood rolled over, as if he didn't want to look. 'Wrong keyhole,' he said. 'They do look the same.'

Henry was beside them now. He wasn't moaning any more. Being back in this world seemed to have done him some good. 'Is this the office place?' he said.

The Dood nodded. 'The Consortium.'

There was a whole minute's silence while the fact sank in.

'OK,' said Enna. 'Let's think. It's in the High Street, right? So we can just walk home.' Very cautiously, she tried the door. Then rattled at it harder. 'Oh,' she said.

'It's locked.' Enna took a breath and thought: now, what would Nico do? 'The window,' she said. Climbing on a desk, then on a filing cabinet, Enna could just reach it. As she pulled her face up level with the glass, she saw that it opened just a crack . . . and then was blocked with iron bars. Security conscious people, the Consortium . . . Some way below, she saw the roofs of houses—her house, Nico's, and the Aspidistras'—Surrey Street. It seemed as distant as another planet.

'Let's not panic,' she said, climbing down. 'Let's be sensible. We aren't trapped. We can always go back . . . through the Margin.' Henry gave a little whimper; the Dood gave a groan.

'The shifty thing,' said Henry. 'Is it . . . waiting?'

'I expect so,' the Dood said. 'Once it gets an idea into its mind, it can wait for, oh, *centuries*.'

'Centuries?' said Enna, bleakly.

'It's got no imagination, you see. None of them have. They're just content to *be imagined*. None of them have got any curiosity.'

'Except you,' said Enna.

'Except me. Just think: a thousand years out there, with neighbours like that! You try and start a conversation, like *What's the meaning of life?* or *Do you regard yourself as a physical or a metaphysical being?* They just stare at you!'

Enna and Henry stared at the Dood. He buried his face in his hands and, Enna thought, began to cry.

'I'm starving,' Henry said.

'Oh, Henry, be quiet,' snapped Enna. 'You're the one who got us into this.'

'There's somebody's lunchbox,' he said, pointing at the table.

'That's stealing . . . ' Enna said, then her stomach rumbled too. They could be here for hours, after all, and what would happen if Henry started whingeing again? 'OK,' she said. 'This is an emergency.'

There were two thin fish paste sandwiches in gritty healthy bread—the kind of thing neither of them would have touched at home. Right now, it was a banquet. They even drank the lukewarm coffee from the thermos, and the world began to seem a slightly better place. Enna sat back, rocking on the swivel chair, and let her eyes track up the wall. And stopped.

The map. The map the Dood had mentioned, with the names and dates and details of the plans for Surrey Street. There it was, on the cork notice board, and only four drawing pins to hold it in place. If Wes could see that, he'd believe her. They wouldn't have to talk about the Dood or anything—this was the evidence, if only she could get it home with her. In half a minute it was rolled up neatly in her hand. Now all they had to do was get out of the building. They had all the evidence they'd need.

That was when they heard the voices. Outside in the office, two men came in, talking. 'Shout!' Henry whispered. 'They'll let us out.'

Enna opened her mouth . . . and shut it. One voice, a big rough one, came a little nearer, and she had a crawling feeling up her spine. She'd heard that voice before, in Surrey Street—yes, that day at the squat, with Wes and Nico. Big Mack, Wes had called him. He was just outside the door.

The other voice, a smooth expensive kind of voice, spoke. 'We need to discuss the next phase in some detail. I'll access the data. Help yourself to a drink. This could be a long evening.'

'No prob,' said the rough voice. 'I got a-a-all the time in the world.'

Enna stared at the door. Trapped. There was no way out of here, except that window. Or back into the Margin, of course, and she knew what was waiting there. The map in her hand felt very big and heavy. Then she saw the phone.

She lifted it down on the floor, beneath the desk, and held it very close. If she spoke, would they hear her from the office? And who should she call? The police? Yes, they were bad guys out there, not much doubt of that, but can you really phone the police and say: Hello, I'm just burgling someone's office, and it's somewhere in the High Street but I don't remember which number the Dood said, and it doesn't matter who the Dood is, there's this map, you see . . . Maybe not. She punched in Mum and Wes's number. And waited. And waited. Now, of all times, why, oh why, oh why . . . They weren't at home.

Who else could she trust? There was one other person. There was a phone book on the filing cabinet. Henry stared at her, speechless, as she riffled through it, fast and very carefully.

Sideriou. Yes! She was huddled down under the desk, and dialling. It was one of the sisters who answered. 'Please,' whispered Enna, 'can I speak to Nico? Quickly!'

'I can't hear you. Who is it? Speak up.'

Enna whispered again. 'Please! NICO!' Then there was a hush. Oh, no, she thought. His stupid sister's gone to tell their parents. She'll think it's some kind of nuisance call . . .

Then there was Nico's voice. 'Nico!' Enna whispered.

'Enna! The whole street's looking for you—the police and everyone. Where are you?'

How Enna got everything she needed into so few words, she never could work out. Or maybe she didn't— she just thought she did. But there was Nico, saying, 'Enna, I can hardly hear you. But you're in one of the office blocks on High Street, and you don't know which one, and . . . How did you get in?'

'Can't say. Trust me,' she said. 'Can you climb up to the car park *really quickly*?'

'Course I can. You know me.'

'Two minutes, then. Look up. I'm going to drop something out of the window. See if you can see which window. And pick it up when I drop it. It's really important. You'll see why . . . '

'Why?'

'No time. Got to go.' Then she was climbing up the filing cabinet, threading the rolled-up map out of the window crack, between the bars. She waited: two minutes, she'd said. Give him a little longer, just a little longer. There were voices again, and the grate of a chair in the office outside. The door of the office rattled, but it didn't open. Locked. But the relief only lasted a second. There was the chink of someone fiddling with his keys.

With one wild effort Enna heaved herself up high enough to squint out through the crack of window . . . and yes, there was the car park, and yes, there was the flash of a sweater she knew. Nico! Trust me, she'd said and he had, in no time. She could hardly stop herself from shouting, *Nico, Nico!* But the key was in the door behind her. 'Enna!' Henry quailed behind her, and she froze.

But the door didn't open. She heard a man swearing under his breath. Wrong key. She waggled the map through the crack, and she was almost sure that Nico looked up, just as she gave it a push and it sailed free. Then she was scrambling down, just as another key creaked in the lock. She dropped on all fours, and as Henry and Enna shrank beneath the table, there were Big Mack's shoes and trousers. The door clicked behind him, and a match struck. Enna froze, her arm round Henry, and she felt him trembling. The Dood shrank in behind them, going as small as he could. Funny, she had the impression it was hard for him—there was *more* of him, somehow. And hadn't she put a hand on his shoulder just now, and really *shaken* him? Now she'd seen and felt him in the Margin, it was hard to think of him being just an outline, in this world.

Where was the photocopied picture? There, across the room, she saw it wedged against the wall.

The man planted his weight on the edge of the table and began to smoke. For a small eternity he dragged at the cigarette, sighed, and a puff of smoke rolled down. It was tickling Enna's throat; she wanted to cough; she bit her lip and held her breath until her eyes watered. Drag, sigh, puff, drag, sigh . . . It was getting faster. Big Mack was impatient, and his big foot tapped and tapped. *Damn it!* With an angry mutter he stubbed out the smoke and dropped it. For a second Enna saw it, falling—a thin brown fag-end, bent at right angles, like the ones Nico and she had seen at the empty house. And the next second it hit Henry's leg.

'Ow!' Henry yelped. Big Mack sprang forward, almost upending the table. He came down into a crouch, and his square face widened in a nasty grin.

'Well, well,' said Big Mack. 'We got mice, have we?' He squinted. 'Don't I recognize you, little girl?'

This was it, thought Enna. She got to her feet. 'Let us out of here,' she said, as bravely as she could. 'Or I'll scream.'

Big Mack looked at her. Then he began to chuckle softly. And the Dood made his move. But as he leaped towards his picture, something happened that Enna would have to replay very slowly in her mind before she'd understand.

There was a kind of impact, a big dull *thud!* and there were two Doods. The one in the room yelped and threw himself backwards as the other hung for a moment just in front of the picture, like a reflection that had come loose from its mirror. Then it started growing . . . and as it grew the Dood-like outlines wavered, sprouting hints of hands and legs and horns, then filling up with curdling, choking smoke.

'The Shifty!' Henry gasped, and Enna got it: yes, it was a shape-shifter, and it had made itself small and Dood-shaped for just long enough . . . It had squeezed through the keyhole, and poured into this world. Now it was through, it could turn into any shape it wanted to. And it was growing as they watched it, feeding on the shock in Henry's voice and the fear in their eyes.

Big Mack spun round and saw it, his size now and snarling, face to face. He lashed out, and the Shifty gave a fiery ripple as the man's anger flowed into its veins. It billowed up and outwards—still a flat thing but billowing, flapping like a red sheet hung out in the wind. It wrapped itself round Big Mack's fist . . . his arm . . . his shoulder, and the two of them were rolling, tangling, cursing on the floor.

'Follow me!' the Dood yelled. He was by his picture, wedging himself into it, stretching the keyhole. Enna and Henry darted for it, as the Dood made one more effort. Big Mack was stumbling backwards now, coughing his lungs out, spitting rage.

'Fire!' he croaked. 'Fire!'

'Inkle!' Enna whispered. 'Can the Shifty follow us?'

'Yes. Can't do anything about it,' the Dood gasped. 'Hurry!'

'What if the picture . . . wasn't here any more?'

'What?' But Enna had reached back on the floor, and she had Big Mack's smouldering cigarette end in her hand. She touched the edge of the paper, stretched around the Dood's outline, and blew, and blew. As it caught fire, she grabbed Henry. 'Ow!' the Dood shrieked, and they jumped.

They jumped together, and they felt the Dood jump

with them, as the flame consumed the paper, with the precious picture. There was a hot rush, as it crisped and flared up round them . . . then was gone. And Enna was falling—free fall, in a whirl of pictures. Enna saw a young monk looking up from his work, his quill pen dropping from his hand—looking up, where a Viking not unlike Big Mack loomed suddenly above him, and the axe came down . . .

'Owwww . . . ' The Dood was moaning.

'Are you OK? Oh, I'm sorry. Did I burn you?' They were lying on the hillside, in the mist and chill.

'A bit. Not as bad as that big man over there is getting burned.'

'I didn't know . . . ' said Henry. 'I didn't know the Shifty was like *that*.'

'It loves violence,' the Dood said. 'You just woke it up. That man—he's violent too—he'll get it really excited.'

'But it can't get back here?' Enna said.

'Not now, without the keyhole. That was clever . . . Good job you didn't ask me, though.'

'Why?'

'I'd have said it was impossible,' the Dood said. 'Now, let's find the *other* keyhole.' He got to his feet, and staggered, and crumpled. 'Sorry,' he said. 'I'm all used up.'

'That's OK,' Enna said. 'We'll carry you.'

Chapter 17

The Evidence

Enna and Henry crumpled on the bedroom floor together. It had been agony, watching the Dood strain every fibre of himself to hold their keyhole open. 'Stretch me . . . ' he'd gasped, and they'd leaned against his outline, though it felt so frail that it might snap. 'Don't stop . . . ' he whispered. 'Now . . . Don't wait for me. Just go!' And they jumped.

'Are you OK?' said Enna. Henry was already on his feet and looking round.

'Where's the Dood?' he said.

'Inkle!' they both called. 'Ink-le!' There was no answer, and the picture looked as small and empty as it had ever been. Seeing it, there was an empty space inside Enna too. But in her head she heard the Dood's voice, his last words to them both: *Don't wait for me.*

He was right. They had to hurry. As long as Nico had the map, he'd be in danger. As soon as they got it into Mum's and Wes's hands, they'd have the evidence they needed to save Surrey Street.

As Enna and Henry hit the landing there was Connie. She stopped stone still, staring, then she screamed. 'Mum! Mum! It's Enna and Henry!' Then an incredible thing: she threw her arms around them both and hugged them tight.

'You're back,' she said. 'I've been so . . . *everybody's*

been so worried? What happened? Did they let you go?'

'They?' Enna said. 'Who?'

'Who? The people who . . . Do you mean there wasn't . . . ? That's what everyone's been saying: somebody kidnapped you, you know, to scare us, get us out of Surrey Street. I've been so frightened . . . ' Connie was big-eyed, breathless. 'I thought they were going to come for me next. Did you just . . . run away, then?'

Enna disentangled herself from the hug. 'I didn't run away,' she said. 'And we weren't kidnapped. We just had to . . . find something. We got back as quickly as we could. It was a long way.'

That was when Mum came running up the stairs. She threw her arms round Henry, then round Enna and Henry, then around all three of them, and held them very tight. After a while she dried her eyes and remembered she was very angry. 'You've got some explaining to do, young lady,' she said to Enna. 'I told you not to get him mixed up in your . . . games. Poor Henry!'

'Mum!' said Henry.

'Yes, love?'

'Enna's a hero,' Henry said.

'But where have you *been*?' They were sitting round the table, the five of the family and Nico slightly apart from the rest of them, looking ill at ease. They were all being as calm and normal as they could. 'The police are looking for you,' Mum said.

'We—It's hard to explain,' said Enna. 'But the main thing is: we've got the map!'

Mum, Wes, and Connie stared at her. 'Map?' said Mum. 'Oh, Enna . . . we've been worried about *you*.'

'No, this is really important,' Enna said.

'Enna, love . . . ' Mum started but Wes made a little gesture. *Let her talk*, it meant. Nico brought out the crumpled roll of paper.

Unrolling it now, it didn't look quite so convincing. Nico had been there—he was just as quick a climber as he'd said—but it had fluttered wildly all the way down; he couldn't catch it. When he got to it, it had been lying in an oily puddle. Still, you could still see the plan of the street, and a lot of the writing, though it all looked faded.

'You said we needed evidence,' she said to Wes.

Mum gave Wes an odd look, but he squinted at the paper. 'Where did you get this?' he said to Nico.

'From their headquarters . . . the people who want to knock the street down,' Enna said. Everything was coming out in the wrong order. 'Nico wasn't there.'

'Then how . . . ?' Wes shook his head.

'I found it in the car park,' Nico said. He was just thinking how to put the next bit. He was running back home to phone the police, and just as he got there the phone went, and it was Enna, breathless, phoning him from home. It seemed like some game she was playing, but her voice had sounded serious, and when he came round to the house he could see the family was dead serious too. He looked at Enna, hoping that she'd help him out.

'You got this from somebody's office?' Mum said. 'You mean you stole it?'

'Not exactly. Well, they want to steal all of Surrey Street. That's not fair, is it?'

'Talk us through this,' Wes said, 'very slowly.'

As she came to the end, she dared to look up, at Mum's face and Wes's. For a while neither of them moved. Then Wes shook his head.

'It *is* true,' Henry said. 'She isn't making it up.'

'No, she isn't,' Wes said. 'I don't know about this . . . Margin business. But the stuff with the Consortium makes sense. It fits.'

'So we tell the police?' said Connie.

'That's the thing. Enna, what they're doing isn't stealing. I mean, it is, in a way, but not according to the law. What they're doing probably isn't even illegal. We can tell the police, but . . . they'll probably say the same as me. And they'll ask where you got this map.'

'I'll show them.' Enna got up and walked across to the window. 'I can work out where it is from here . . . ' As she came to the window Enna had a funny feeling, as if her words were coming true in advance. She could have sworn she heard the siren of a police car. No, more than one. And maybe fire engines too.

By the time the family got out on the pavement, half of Surrey Street was there. Up over the backs of the houses, in the High Street, there was smoke with blue lights flashing in it, and all kinds of sirens. Soon someone in the crowd passed round the rumour. It was one of the office blocks up there—a really nasty fire, the word was. Might be accident, or might be arson. The fire brigade were getting people out, somebody said. Enna glanced at Henry, and saw the same uneasy look in his eyes. Big Mack . . . They'd left him in there with the Shifty. Yes, he was a bad guy, but . . . ?

'Has anyone been hurt?' said Enna.

Mum gave her an odd look. 'Not badly, by the sound of it. There were only a couple of blokes in there— working late, I guess. They were lucky.'

Enna's sick feeling was passing. She didn't like to think of Big Mack burnt to cinders. Was it OK, she wondered, though, to hope that he'd been scared out of his big nasty bullying wits, so he'd never come back here, ever?

She sat alone in her room, staring at her doodle on its page. They'd sent Nico home, without so much as thanking him for everything he'd done. No one had said much when she'd talked about the Dood, and nobody had looked her in the eye. Worst of all, they hadn't even let her talk to Nico, to make sure he believed her. He knew she'd been in the office, at least—he'd seen the map falling. As for the others . . . maybe they thought she was making it all up, her and Henry. And maybe that was better. People would be asking questions about the fire.

If only the Dood had been there with them, that would have cleared it all up, and they'd all believe her, easy. But the Dood was gone.

Henry tried to tell her that he was probably just feeling shy again, but with a feeling deep inside her Enna knew. The drawing on the paper had never looked so completely deserted—like so many houses looked in Surrey Street. She had tried to think, she had tried calling him out loud, she'd even tried getting angry like she had the first time, but she didn't feel the slightest quiver of reaction on the page. The Dood was gone. With a chilly feeling she remembered his voice, growing fainter, as they'd struggled through the Margin. *I'm all used up*, he'd said. And she had left him in there . . . Enna tried to stop the cold thought forming, but she couldn't. Had she left him there to die?

There was a tap on the door. 'Enna . . . ' said Connie from behind her. 'I just wanted to say . . . you were brave . . . whatever really happened.'

'Don't you believe us, then?'

'I don't know. Everybody thinks you had a kind of . . . *trauma*, they keep saying. And that it made you imagine things. Enna . . . ' Connie paused, embarrassed. 'I didn't think you'd been kidnapped. I thought maybe you'd run away, because of me.'

'Of *you*?' said Enna.

'I haven't been very nice to you,' said Connie. 'And another thing . . . ' She squirmed again. 'I think you're right. I mean, I don't want to spend my life in this place, but some of what's been happening—the old lady, and the squat—well, it's not right.'

'Are you going to join Jenny's campaign, then?'

Connie wrinkled her face. 'Oh, God, what if anybody *saw* me?'

'You could wear disguise. Some hippy stuff, you know . . . '

'Yuck!' Connie paused. 'Mum says I should look after Henry so you don't . . . you know, *lead him on* . . . '

'Me? Lead *him* on? Huh!'

'I know.' Connie grinned at her. 'I just wondered if you'd like to come out. Hang out for a bit. I mean, when everyone has calmed down. We could go to see the Aspidistras.'

Enna stared at her. 'And Henry?' Connie nodded. 'And can we take Nico too?'

'Wes thinks he got you into—whatever you've been doing.'

'No way. He doesn't believe in the Dood. But I've got to have him there . . . please! Anyway, we need everyone who cares about Surrey Street. Sounds like Mum and Wes are giving up.'

'If this is a council of war,' said Maggie Aspidistra, 'we'd better go somewhere private.'

Four extra people in the Glory Box—Connie, Henry, Enna, and Nico—filled every corner, even when they all stood up. They kept losing Henry in piles of sheepskin coats. Maggie threaded a passage through the racks and out the back. A step across the yard and scents of incense hit them: they were in the lean-to, Maggie's meditation room. It was almost as private in there as in Nico's cave . . . and there was the same hanging curtain of ivy. The sisters had left the ivy trailing down the rock wall, inside, parting it in one place like an alcove, where a thick white candle waited in a blue glass bowl. Nico looked round, in case there was a broomstick, but all he saw was cushions and a couple of low stools.

'No clutter,' Maggie said. 'We come out here to think.' And thinking was what they needed, everyone agreed. Maggie lit the candle.

'If Wes is right,' said Jenny, 'then the police can't stop them. But there are planning regulations, things like that. If only we had a historic building, say, they wouldn't be allowed to knock it down.'

'The café's pretty ancient?' Connie said.

'Not the right sort of old. It's a pity we haven't got your Inkle here, Enna, to advise us.' Enna touched the paper in her bag—she'd been doing that a lot just recently, hoping for that slight tickle of something moving—but it only felt like paper.

'Inkle?' Nico said. 'Who's Inkle?' Enna didn't answer. Just then, she felt her nose prickling with the smell of smoke.

'What's wrong with that candle?' Maggie said. But it wasn't the candle.

Suddenly Henry clutched at Enna, whimpering. 'No! The Shifty!'

'Sshhh,' she put an arm around him. 'It's miles away. It'll be back in the Margin. It . . . ' The thought hit her. Where could it go, after they burned the Dood's keyhole? It couldn't get back. What else could it do, but try and find them? It was *over here*.

Under the door, a thin low seep of smoke was flowing in like water, with a hissing sound. At first it lay flat on the ground, then suddenly it stood up on end, streaming, snapping out sideways like a battle flag. Connie screamed.

The Shifty drank in her fear and a flush of sparks rushed upwards through its straining shape. Everyone was getting to their feet and stumbling, coughing, and the Shifty hung there, with an angry orange glow inside. *Inkle!* thought Enna, *Inkle* . . . What would the Dood say, if he were here?

'Don't look at it,' she said, as firmly as she could. But how could you not look? 'Don't pay it attention.'

But the others did. As they stared, the thing was rising, spreading, sprouting, and shuffling its shapes as they watched. With one sweep of its head it touched the candle with an antler tip. The little flame flared, as bright as a bonfire, and its smoke and fire poured back to join the Shifty, which looked almost solid now, wrapping its cloak of fire round and round itself, swelling up and feeding on their fear. It was rippling all over, like horrible muscles, and there was a hard bright blade of fire inside. One part of it blocked the doorway, while another part moved forward, slowly, towards one of them, then the next.

Henry clutched at Enna, sobbing almost without sound. It was enough, though, and the smoke thing heard him. It swivelled sharply, and was creeping forward. 'Stop it!' Enna shouted. 'It wants Henry!' Nico lashed out at it and jumped back, cradling a scalded fist. Connie crept the other side of Henry, trying to cover him, but the thing seeped forward.

'Enna!' Nico called. 'Your bag!'

Enna looked. The bag, just out of reach beside her, was bulging and writhing. 'Open it!' she said, and Nico leaped for it. The Shifty's sixth or seventh arm lunged at him, but he ducked and wriggled on, on hands and knees. Now he was fumbling with the bag, with its awkward stiff catch, and the smoke whooshed down around him. For a moment there was only coughing and struggling in there, then the smoke parted—a shape in the smoke, growing larger, clearer—and there, as real and solid as Enna had ever seen him this side of the Margin, was the Dood.

He faced the Shifty. 'Come on, smoke-head, soot-face, bonfire-brain!' the Dood was taunting. 'Pick on somebody your own size for a change!' He tossed down his picture behind him, and it landed propped against the wall. The Dood took up a stance in front of it, a bit like a goalkeeper guarding a very small goal.

'You think you're hot stuff, do you?' he jeered. For a moment the Shifty reeled back, into the candle-alcove, gathering its fire in and coiling to strike. 'Hot air,' scoffed the Dood. 'Come on then, let's have you!'

As the fire thing flared to white hot rage, the ivy round it caught fire in a crackling whoosh, like a whole box of fireworks going off at once. The flames ran up looped strands of ivy, crisping and coiling them, throwing off sparks so bright that Enna had to shield her eyes. It was as if the Shifty had burst in its anger, blown itself apart. For a second there was silence, and in the dark of her head all Enna saw were burning after-images, scribbles of cave-things, leaping hunters and stampeding animals and the half-men-half-beasts dancing in between.

Only the Dood didn't flinch. He was crouched by his

piece of paper, taunting, making playground faces at the place where the Shifty had been.

Enna opened her eyes. Nothing there. It had gone. She looked round at the others, who were looking round, blinking. But why was the Dood still behaving as if . . .

Whoosh. Imagine that grand-finale box of fireworks in reverse. Those last faint drifting sparks, the wisps of smoke . . . twitch and run backwards, flow into each other, *flash*, with a star-burst inwards, then pouring back down to the ground, together. So the bits of scattered Shifty wriggled and coiled, like fire snakes, down the burnt-out ivy. Everyone screamed, and there it was, person-sized but incandescent, drinking their panic . . . then turning to face the Dood with antlers lowered, crackling with white hot flame.

The Dood didn't budge. They were the same size now, but he was stretched, Enna could tell, while the Shifty was condensed down to the smallest brightest shape she'd ever seen. It was no match. But the Dood was cackling. 'Who's a damp squib? Ner-ner-nerner-ner . . . '

And the Shifty sprang.

As it swooped, the Dood stepped back, back, and as he stepped he shrank in, in towards his picture, till he touched it—an exact fit. *He's going back through the keyhole*, Enna thought, and the Shifty, in whatever brain it had, thought it too, because it was shrinking with him, moulding itself to Dood-shape and at almost exactly the moment the Dood leaped back through it followed.

It was hardly a second before the picture quivered, and there was the Dood, his small neat shape, again. No sooner had he touched the ground than he picked up the paper—his own keyhole—and he ripped it in half, then in halves of those halves, then several times again.

Enna stared at him. 'Inkle, what have you done?'

'I'd get rid of those pieces,' he said to Maggie. He'd come up to medium size now, much like Enna's. It might have been the way he'd wrapped his wings around him, but in this light, Enna thought, he could almost pass for human. A bit short and gnarled, but . . .

Henry looked out between Connie and Enna. 'Has the Shifty . . . has it really gone?' he said.

'It's out there in the Margin,' said the Dood. 'Don't worry, it can't get back now. Not here, anyway. You've seen the last of it.'

The others gave a little sigh and Nico gave a cheer. But Enna wasn't cheering.

'Oh, Inkle,' she said. 'That was your only keyhole.'

There was a hush. 'Well . . . ' the Dood said, trying to sound casual, 'it wouldn't be a good idea, right now. It's a pretty small-minded thing, your Shifty. It'll be angry for a long time.'

'How long?' Enna said.

'Oh, a couple of centuries.'

'What will you do?' said Enna. 'You said you couldn't live . . . you know, *over here.*'

The Dood looked round them slowly. 'That would be true,' he said, 'if no one thinks I'm real. But you seem to think I am. If all the others think so too . . . maybe I can be?'

Looking back later, Enna thought that maybe everything hung on that next moment. What if one of them had blinked and said, *I'm seeing things, this can't be true*? Instead, there was a hush, then Nico got up and went over to the Dood, and shook him by the hand.

'Hey,' Maggie Aspidistra said. 'Look at the wall!' They all looked. On the bare rock of the alcove, just where the Shifty had flared up, as bright as lightning, there were scorch marks. Not pictures exactly, but like a trace of the after-images Enna'd seen inside her dazzled eyes—the leaping animals, the birds in flight, the savage dancers, and the antlered man. Jenny went over, rather gingerly, and touched one of the marks with her finger. The soot did not come off.

'Hot stuff,' she said. 'It's burned right in to the rock.' She stood back and admired the figures, her head on one side.

'This reminds me of something,' she said, almost to herself. 'Cave paintings . . . You know—stylized shapes—part human, part animal—and those fantastic sketchy lines—more like how they move than just a picture. I saw them once, in North Africa. Awesome . . . ' Then, with a big smile: 'I think I've got an idea . . . '

Chapter 18

A Grand Opening

On the night the Surrey Street cave paintings opened
to the public, there was a big do, with the press and all.
It had taken some time, of course, because the experts—
archaeologists, anthropologists, art historians—all had to
study it in depth. It was lucky that Jenny Aspidistra's
nephew was a research student at the museum, or who
would even have bothered to look when some unknown
people said this incredible thing, that they had uncovered
a Stone Age site right in the middle of the city,
overlooked for all these years? But there were carbon-
dating tests and though the dates weren't certain, they
were certainly extremely old. Professors were preparing
books on it already.

They'd had to install a glass screen
to protect the painting, which Maggie
thought was a shame. She still wanted
to come and meditate in here
sometimes, and the bare rock made
her feel at one with the earth, she used
to say. But everyone agreed the public
ought to see it.

Now, though, there was music. Wes
had agreed to play his guitar in public,
for the first time, and it sounded more
mellow and sweet than anyone had
ever heard, behind the chatter. Jenny
and Mum went round with trays of

Mum's own cooking, and the man from the Council told some people from the press that he didn't know much about archaeology but this was just the kind of enterprise the city needed. A community effort, too: after visiting the paintings, people could get their Mammoth-burgers and Rock buns in the Cave Café, just a few doors up, or a whole range of souvenirs from the corner shop. Nico had put that idea to his uncle, who was suddenly looking at him with a new expression on his face. This wasn't his fond but rather lazy nephew but a young man with a sound business plan, who would probably do great things with the shop one day. Most important of all, there was no question of anyone being allowed to pull down Surrey Street.

'Hey,' Nico came up close behind Enna. 'Like your hat!' She'd got dressed up, for once. Jenny had offered her the pick of the Glory Box to go with the velvet hat, but very tactfully Enna said that Connie had already offered to take her shopping in the High Street. Connie needed new things for the evening, because Jenny's nephew would be there. He was twenty-three and *Well*, said Connie in a whisper, *isn't he gorgeous? Do you think I stand a chance?*

At the height of the evening there were photographs in front of the painting. As the group broke up, Mr Sideriou came over to where Nico and Enna were standing back, on the fringes, watching it all and smiling.

'A fine night, princess,' he said to Enna. 'I have a message for you. Little man over in the corner, you know? In the big coat with the buttons . . . '

Maggie glanced back over her shoulder. 'Vintage 1968,' she said. 'I knew we'd find a home for it eventually.'

Nico's uncle slipped a folded piece of paper into Enna's hand. 'Said he was most sorry, but he had to be leaving for a journey.'

As Mr Sideriou turned away Enna opened the note and saw the crinkly old-world scrawl. 'Oh . . . ' she said. Nico gave her hand a little squeeze.

'Best let him go,' he whispered, and she nodded. She'd guessed what she'd see on the note before she'd read it.

GONE TO LINDISFARNE, it said.